AEGEAN

AEGEAN NIGHTS AEGEAN DAYS

The Secret Diaries of The Hon. Edward Andersonn

JAVELIN BOOKS
POOLE · NEW YORK · SYDNEY

First published in the UK 1987 by Javelin Books,
Link House, West Street, Poole, Dorset, BH15 1LL

Distributed in the United States by
Sterling Publishing Co., Inc.,
2 Park Avenue, New York, NY 10016

Distributed in Australia by
Capricorn Link (Australia) Pty Ltd,
PO Box 665, Lane Cove, NSW 2066

British Library Cataloguing in Publication Data

Andersonn, Edward
Aegean nights, Aegean days: the secret
diaries of the honourable Edward Andersonn.
I. Title
823'914[F]   PR6051.N4

ISBN 0 7137 1904 4

Typeset by Butler & Tanner Ltd,
Frome and London
Printed in Great Britain
by Hazell Watson and
Viney Ltd, Aylesbury

1 September 1920.
I have been mulling over one of those paragraphs I wrote yesterday.

> and knowing that Lina had not been satisfied, I asked her to lie on her back against me again, curled together, and this time I reached my hand around her waist and placed my fingers inside her, finding her moist pearl, which I touched and caressed until she reached her own climax, and grabbed my wrist to stop me fingering her at the same time as she yelled and bit into the pillow....
>
> So we stayed. And we were so close it was as if we slept each other's sleep.

And now, with Lina naked and asleep on the wooden bed behind me, I will read again from the beginning. Six months is not a long time in the life of a man, but it seems I have travelled further than I knew in that short time.

18 March, 1920

The other Englishman, Henry something-something, was complaining again at breakfast about the bed-bugs. I do sympathise, but complaints of that nature are not what I want to hear when trying to eat – at least, not for five minutes and more. I teased him a little, which was perhaps not the wisest way to react, and said I saw a tiny creature hop onto his hot bread, whereupon he proceeded to dismantle the loaf and scatter coarse crumbs across the table, much to the puzzlement of Ianni, our waiter.

Ianni has been a hotel waiter for many years, and must by now be used to the peculiarities of foreign behaviour, especially that of the English, but to see a respectable guest rip apart a piece of fresh bread so as to cover the wooden table-top in crumbs which in their turn were picked up and peered at, must have been a new experience. I thought I detected a quizzical lift in his eyebrow, which in itself counts, no doubt, almost as hysteria in Ianni's phlegmatic expression.

As yet my experience of the Greeks is naturally limited, but they are in general undoubtedly a lively and demonstrative race. Not Ianni. His visage has the immobility of a glacier. He looks as much a part of this old hotel as that incongruous grandfather clock in the lobby. I wonder what is the Greek for 'Grandfather clock'? Do they even have that same expression? I could have asked Henry his opinion, but that would only have lead inexorably to a tirade against the local attitude to time-keeping, which I suffered yesterday.

Unfortunately for Henry, who has been travelling around this complex country for some weeks, the only time any form of public transport has left on time has been on those very occasions when he himself was a few minutes late. (I shall name this Henry's Law.)

Henry asked me today if I wished to accompany him to the Acropolis, and such a visit had indeed been my plan, having now passed my first few days in exploring the geography of the incredible city.

I have been saving the Acropolis and the Parthenon, and I think I shall save it further. Henry is a hurried walker, and though I no longer need a stick my slight limp is a little too troublesome for his pace. I feel slightly guilty and unfriendly as I tell him that I have appointments to keep, but I do not wish my first sight of the Acropolis to be forever associated in my mind with Henry whining about the heat, the cold, the climb, the people or his flea-bites. I do not doubt that much of the magic of such a moment would be lost, and having seen precious little of life's magic in the past few years, perhaps a little selfishness might be forgiven.

It seemed not to occur to Henry to wonder what appointments I might have here, a young Englishman just arrived on his first visit to Athens knowing absolutely no-one in the strange country, but he accepted my explanation without comment. I feel sure I could have invented appointments if necessary. There are endless forms to complete, bank drafts to arrange and officials to visit.

I am writing this entry while indulging in my first appointment of the day, one which I can see is going to become a regular mid-day event! With a bottle of local wine and some food. The cost of everything is so remarkably reasonable here that it seems my remittance from England could last a lifetime. I passed the morning walking the clustered back streets, still thrilled at the sight of this bustling and busy city.

Those French towns were also delightful, and yet always how strange and unreal it used to be to enjoy food and good wine while knowing that the Germans or the Austrians were but a few miles away and that I would soon be returning to face the trenches. Sometimes memory returns, conjured up by a sight, a smell, a sound, and a shiver passes over me as a cloud's shadow does in the sunshine.

The restaurant is situated on what I believe from my map to be Constitution Square, although the reading of maps was never one of my strongest subjects. I have started to try to master again the Greek alphabet, which should at least enable me to read street signs, and perhaps then I can start to learn something more of the language itself, which I shall certainly require once I move outside the city. Thankfully English is quite surprisingly widespread here.

It pleases me that I can sit and read, or watch the world walking by, with no hint from the waiters that I ought to be ordering something more to eat or drink, which would surely be the case in England. Before ordering my grilled fish I had been sitting here with nothing but a glass of water and a cup of the thick local coffee, a concoction so cheap that they might as well simply give it away (although judging by the expression of visitors when they first encounter this strong bitter taste, even to give it away might not be so simple). I am, however, determined to persist with

Greek food and drink, for how can one understand a country without experiencing what the people experience, eating what they eat and drinking what they drink?

The coffee, it seems, is generally served without sugar, and I am sure that the waiters derive some satisfaction from seeing visitors take their first sip – faces as if they had both bitten into a lemon and simultaneously smelled something vile. Only today I heard an English woman say to her husband, 'It's such an *interesting* taste, isn't it, Neville?'

Fortunately I have learned how to ask for a cup with a small amount of sugar included, rendering it slightly more palatable.

Equally 'interesting' is the taste of the famous resinated Greek wine, which I shall certainly be investigating. In my first few days here I have sampled several varieties, some hardly resinated at all and so almost passable as a pleasant and light white wine; while others, taken straight from the barrel in the small back street taverns, are so strong as to be comparable to a piece of alcoholic pine bark, if such a thing be imaginable.

I have heard several English and American voices in the course of the past few days, but as yet I have done nothing about attempting to converse with anybody. I feel solitude is a state to be savoured at the moment, but only acceptable, perhaps, because of the knowledge that it can be broken at any time. I could pass my days with Henry, and put up with the weight of his conversation for the sake of company or the occasional useful nuggets of information with which he provides me. A strange chap – upright, English, punctilious and punctual, yet still wishing to spend weeks travelling in a country where the political situation is chaotic and disorder is prevalent; but we all have our own reasons and our own lives to lead.

At the other side of this restaurant, in the next restaurant along, sit a laughing group of three young women, all blonde, with healthy outdoor faces; all talking to each other, animatedly and confidently, in what sounds to me to be a Scandinavian tongue. Only the occasional word reaches me amidst the noise of the Greek diners and passers-by.

No solitude for those three. They have the look of people who are at home here, or who have at least been here for some weeks or months. I cannot explain why I should assume this, except for a certain casual familiarity in the way that, despite black glances from the street, the waiter remains and talks to them at some length. They must speak Greek to some extent, although it is hard to hear in the noise. Something else I have discovered about Greece is that while a meal here can sometimes be almost an assault on one's taste, it is always an assault on the eardrums! From the amount that the people here eat, and the way that they voraciously attack the food, it might seem inevitable that much of the meal should be taken in silence, the mouths of all fully occupied with their food. Yet every table is surrounded by a babble of talk and argument. How I enjoy it, thinking back to sombre silent meals spent around the dining table at home, as if food were to be endured rather than enjoyed.

The three women have paid up and left, and walk purposefully along the square and around a corner, much too briskly to be merely taking in the sights. I shall pay too and find a piece of grassy shade somewhere to read Dante. It is pleasingly warm for March, although I expect it is still snowing in England.

19 March

I went down to breakfast a couple of hours earlier today, hoping to escape Henry, but he joined me shortly afterwards, in an attempt to escape the bed bugs. I would have taken his word for it without him baring his chest at me over the yoghurt and honey. Ianni looked on, as impassively as ever.

Yesterday Henry complained to the manager of the hotel about the bugs but, it seems, the manager refused to acknowledge their existence, despite all visual evidence to the contrary. I do find it hard to believe that anything animate or inanimate could get past him without being handed a bill. Henry has my sympathy, and it seems he also has my bugs, for I have certainly never been troubled by them here. As I write this now, by the lamplight in my room, I can see and hear no evidence of unwelcome intruders. God knows, I saw enough vermin at the front. The hotel is cheap even by Athenian standards, but so far I have found it clean. I am expecting to sleep in many worse places before my escapade is over.

To escape from the subject of bugs, about which I am sure Henry would have talked for the rest of the morning if permitted, reliving every bite, I asked him about his visit to the great Acropolis. It seems remarkable that on this topic he has considerably less to say for himself.

I realise Henry is about to get into his stride when he reaches the subject of surrounding squalor and the noisy disorderly crowds, but as by this time I have finished my breakfast I tell him quickly that I must leave to reach the ruins before too many others are about. He asks how my meetings went, and I tell him it was a case of waiting at the bank for several hours for confirmation of the arrival of some money. He nods sympathetically, and I leave him confirmed in his certainty that all Englishmen were born to suffer at the hands of others.

I have not as yet fulfilled my promise to myself to wake and go out onto the streets in the extreme early morning, to watch the city come alive with its inhabitants – if indeed there is ever a moment during the night when the city is not alive. Perhaps in the hour between three and four there might be a brief lull when those going home do not overlap with those rising to go to work.

By eight this morning the city was fully awake, and the sun was rising in the sky as I walked towards the distant Acropolis, which stood golden and impressive over Athens like a king overlooking his kingdom – or perhaps a queen, its contours and lines in the early sunlight looking decidedly smooth. Soft even, almost feminine and far less angular than I expected.

For a time, in the almost mediaeval clutter of streets at the foot of the Acropolis, the building itself becomes invisible, the map useless, and I rely on directions from people who know where the visitor must be heading. Certainly not to see them, the unshaven men in their dusty workshops and the dark-eyed women sitting watchful in the doorways of their small homes, already preparing vegetables for the midday meal. A city of contrasts – doubtless not an original observation, but none the less true. Other visitors keep their gaze averted from the poverty all too evident around them, yet what dramas of life must be acted out behind those shopfronts and doorways?

How can I describe the sight that greets the eyes? The Parthenon itself is familiar now from picture postcards and paintings, yet as you pick your way over the rocks of the Acropolis and the vast stones loom before you, it is as if you are seeing something magical for the first time, something so beautiful as to be not of this earth. Its lines are perfect, and it is said, I do not know how truly, that there is not one straight line in the entire building.

As I walked between the vast pillars, I could swear I felt the restless ghosts surrounding me. Though the site was busy, crowded with people in modern dress, I found this fancy only added a strong feeling of continuity to my already strong expectation of history.

I remained on the site for part of the morning, examined the statues and visited the small museum, then sat on one of the old walls nearby resting my aching leg as I looked out at the patchwork city below. It looked like a sprawling ant's nest, full of life and fresh activity. And yet all the talk is of a war with Turkey, and as easily as stamping on an ant's nest, the vital life of the great city could be disrupted, even extinguished.

To turn to more pleasurable things for, goodness knows, I am entitled to some pleasure in my life! I slowly made my way down again, back into the ant's nest, and headed for the restaurant I favour in what (I established by my map-reading today) is certainly Constitution Square. Passing by the adjacent restaurant, however, I noticed the same three young women who were dining there yesterday. One, in particular, with a round face and short fair hair, looked up, half-smiled and then quickly looked away again as I walked in front of their table. I sat down at a near-by table, partly because the women were all three very attractive, but also in the hope that I could overhear their conversation so that I could satisfy my own curiosity about them. Even if their native language was incomprehensible, there was the chance that they might speak in English to the waiters, who attended to them with the diligence one might expect would be given to three unattached foreign women.

I deliberately chose a seat facing their table, facing the one who had chanced to glance up at me, and while I was examining the menu I could hear the sound of what they were saying quite clearly, though I was none the wiser as to what it meant or which country they came from. I thought they might have been speaking Danish or Swedish, though it could equally well have been Norwegian or even Dutch, for all the sense the strange vowel sounds made to me. It was not German, of that at least I was sure.

When the time came for them to order their meal, they each spoke for the most part in Greek, but occasionally with a little English and occasionally pointing at the menu. Quite fluent Greek, it seemed to me, for they spoke in whole sentences, and appeared to understand the greater part of the waiter's replies. Workers here? I wondered. Students of some kind? The waiter hurried across from them to take my own order and, seeing that I was willing to talk, spoke in quite good English of the local wine, the exceptionally good weather and, with a fierce grin, of the trouble now facing the tottering Ottoman empire. I took the opportunity to ask him about the young women.

'Beautiful, yes?' he whispered to me, a fact I had already established for myself.

'From Denmark,' he said 'students of old ... I not know the English, you speak to them, they will tell you.' I nodded my thanks, and said that I would, as he turned and walked back through the crowded restaurant, already shouting his orders to a cook who stood behind a vast black range at the rear of the inside dining room.

I have not the least idea what the waiter said to the women when he eventually brought them their food, but they all looked at me and the smallest of the three smiled, while the one who had been sitting with her back towards me turned to wave. How much more relaxed – no nonsensical formal introduction, no informal introductions, no infernal English stuffiness. I smiled in return and vowed to speak to them before they should leave, which I did, to my great pleasure.

I apologised first of all for the intrusion, but they smiled and did not appear to see it in that light at all. I think they were amused by my hesitant politeness, my Englishness. Much as I hate formality in my fellows and try to fight against it in myself, it is difficult to escape from a lifetime of constriction.

The women all spoke almost faultless English, and it made me once again ashamed of my lack of foreign languages. No matter, the women are indeed Danish, childhood friends from just outside Copenhagen, and are here in Athens to study and work at a private archaeological school. They told me the name but it was equally lengthy and unmemorable in Danish, English and Greek. They apologised, in their turn, for the fact that they had to leave to attend a lecture. And they hoped, they said, that they would see me again.

'Perhaps this evening,' I suggested, but they had already made arrangements. However, we have agreed to meet at lunchtime again tomorrow, at the same restaurant. And after the pleasure of five minutes in their lively company the remainder of the afternoon seemed to pass very quickly. Was it only yesterday I was blessing the benefits of solitude? It is incredible how one smile from a pretty face can change one's outlook so readily.

I was in such a good mood this evening that I even accepted Henry's invitation to dine with him, and commiserated as he recounted how he was overcharged for some kind of insect balm in a back street shop. He doubted very much if it would work. This disappointment appears to have been the high point of his day; being overcharged for an item that would probably turn out to be useless in any case. I wonder if he is being bitten even now?

20 March

I sit in the sun in a quiet park and write, read and think. Pleasures I am beginning to accept might be here to stay. I am almost *willing* lunchtime to arrive, for then I will meet the three women again. Seeing them yesterday and talking to them even briefly, has set me to thinking. About my previous lack of contact with women, for one thing. Perhaps this spring in Greece is a new beginning in that direction. I can only hope so.

I certainly hope that by the end of my time here I have at least one experience which improves on that summer just before the war. Sitting here and looking at sunlight spilling down through the rustling leaves has brought it back, and now I will try to write it – this incident about which I have been allowing myself to think.

This diary must contain all of my moods and thoughts, my secret feelings and observations, whatever is in my mind or memory when I sit down to write, whatever it is that prompts me to write. I will try to be brutally honest and there should be no shame or embarrassment about that. Sometimes it is good to force oneself to own up to true thoughts.

At home this mask is the face you see – politeness dictates that. In France, too, true feelings were often concealed for so long that many broke under the weight.

No, what I have been remembering is the memory of a cousin of mine, Agnes, who came to spend a week with us when I was, I think, fifteen and she perhaps nearly a year older. From what I have learned of mother since, I might be convinced that she was doing a little early matchmaking, were it not for the fact that Agnes and I were rather too closely related for that. I would love now to know why she came to stay – at that age I just accepted it without stopping to consider that she had never been before, or considering afterwards that she has never been since.

It was obviously intended that I should be a good companion for Agnes, a strong-willed, slightly plump girl who certainly had a wild streak of naughtiness in her. The first few days were spent in family outings, I remember, and then I was instructed to show Agnes the delights of our land and of the local countryside, the walks inaccessible to motor-car or carriage. Agnes was what my mother would call a lively young girl, and amusing; she teased me a great deal, asking knowingly about the local girls, and about life at a school where there were only boys. She teased me also in other ways.

On her last afternoon with us, a glorious, endless summer day, she expressed a wish to walk by the riverside, along the stretch that flows swiftly through my father's property. (I will not bring myself to think of it as 'his' river.) We sat near each other at the bottom of the secluded bank and dabbled our legs in the clear water, having only the water beetles for company.

Agnes ordered me to close my eyes. She was forever instructing me to stand here or go there while she secretly prepared some joke or hung some daisy chain around my neck. She would tell me haughtily to open my mouth and close my eyes, and would then surprise me with a sweet or a blackberry: though I could never be certain she would not eventually decide to try something more unpleasant.

On this occasion I closed my eyes, and Agnes promptly told me I could close my mouth too. I heard a swish of bushes and the crunch of dry bracken as she moved behind me. My eyes seemed to be closed forever, but when I asked she only told me to wait and to keep my eyes firmly closed. Eventually she said 'Nearly ready', there was a loud splash and, when she told me I could look, I opened my eyes to see her in the river, evidently quite naked but crouched down so the swift water reached to her shoulders. She was concealed in part by the swirling of the current and its refractions, which broke the outline of her body into a wavering jigsaw.

Was she too daring? she asked, seeming to need to think herself sophisticated, despite her many childish ways. And then I was invited to join her, if I wasn't too scared.

I thought briefly of the likelihood of our being discovered, which was extremely slim, and then hurried behind a wild rhododendron bush to undress – one which concealed most of myself but gave me the chance to watch Agnes as she swam. The water acted as concealment for as long as her feet remained firmly on the river-bed, but as soon as she began to move she revealed to me her smooth glistening back and curved bottom. I could feel myself to be rapidly growing aroused as I pulled my shirt up over my head and stood there quite naked in the open air. We kept horses and I was well aware of the mechanics of physical intimacy, though I had not yet experienced it for myself, and consequently my arousal embarrassed me; especially so when Agnes shouted for me to join her and not be so shy.

I told her crossly that she had to close her eyes and, when she did so, I rushed down the steep bank and threw myself into the river as quickly as possible, for I knew her eyes would not remain closed for long.

I did, I think, manage to reach the icy water before she looked again, but I wish she had warned me how cold it was – I was partly thankful for the chill, however, as it wasn't merely my breath which the coldness of the river took away.

As we swam and splashed at each other, I enjoyed the glimpses I caught of Agnes' body – she had a voluptuous figure for one still young, and I could not hope to hide from her the way my eyes were constantly drawn to her full breasts as they lifted and fell with her movements. Agnes did not object, merely feigned not to notice. We were both, I think, pretending all was innocent, while knowing it was exactly the opposite.

How could it be innocent, when I dived beneath the water to try to hook her legs from under her, only to find my face a few inches from her firm breasts and taut nipples as she ducked down to push me away? Or found close to my mouth a tangle of black hair that swayed in the water like a clump of shimmering ferns moved by the current?

After a good few minutes, Agnes hauled herself out and up the bank, and I watched her curved, rather plump bottom disappear behind the rhododendron bush. I swam some more until she emerged again, not fully dressed as I had expected, but wearing just a white cotton petticoat. Instead of being tied around the waist she had hitched this up and tied it above her breasts as the Malays wear their sarongs, so that it covered her to her knees rather than her ankles; or at least was intended to cover her, for the water from her body had dampened the thin cloth and made it almost transparent.

I decided that shyness was silly, and when I began to tire of swimming against the current I pulled myself out up the bank and sat beside her. She asked slightly uncertainly if I wasn't going to cover myself, so I asked if she objected to me the way I was, and she said that she did not. Then she lay back in the sunshine to dry, while I gazed at the two curves of still-damp cloth stuck to her breasts, and felt myself grow hard again. We were chatting about something, and when she turned her head to speak she could not fail to see that I had become excited.

She said quite bluntly that I could take her if I liked, but it would have to be standing up to avoid her having a baby. Friends at school had told her this in secret: the things one was capable of believing, even those few short years ago. She seemed so sure of her facts that I accepted them. I was not to be allowed to stare at her, though, because she was a bit podgy.

'Come on then,' she said, 'if you want to,' and she stood up, and I stood before her, and we kissed in a very clumsy manner – more a case of bumping our mouths together. I could feel her stomach against mine, her thighs pushing hard against me in a rocking motion. I slid my fingers to her bottom and cupped her flesh in my hands. My shaft was hard but the kissing was a strange sensation, almost sexless, as if we were merely experimenting like children many years younger than ourselves. I put my hand to her breast and felt her nipple harden. Agnes grabbed my penis clumsily and, as it softened, said 'It's not very hard, is it?' Scarcely surprising, as her grip was painful and the situation was hardly the most romantic.

'Put it in me,' she ordered, and lifted her petticoat at the front. I was stooping slightly anyway, but as she was several inches in height shorter than myself, I lowered myself a little further. But when I held my shaft and pushed it in against her still damp hair, trying to find that entrance I knew to be there, I felt myself growing soft not harder.

Without a word, but with a sigh that spoke volumes, Agnes retreated to the rhododendron bush to get dressed and I lay back on the thick carpet of grass and looked up at the sunlight that lit the leaves over my head.

21 March

I have spent some time yesterday considering my immediate plans. Staying in Athens has been pleasant, and I can imagine returning, but the whole summer and the rest of the country stretches before me, and if I am to justify receiving father's continued remittances I must make some attempts to visit the classical sites that are my alleged reason for coming here. I would like to keep my own pension and savings intact for my return to Oxford in the autumn, though it seems a long way away when sitting in a park enjoying the warmth of the sun. (I overheard an English couple complaining of the weather conditions at home on their departure by rail several days ago.) Athens is also expensive (by comparison with the rest of Greece), and while I have at least sufficient for this present visit, I think perhaps I should wait to see how much money I have in hand towards the end of the summer and then arrange to spend an appropriate amount of time back in the city. The cost of food and accommodation elsewhere in Greece is said to be next to nothing, and father's remittances would keep me comfortably for as long as I wish.

And there is the question of Anna. As arranged, I met all three women at the restaurant yesterday to have our midday meal together, and I have not passed such an enjoyable hour or two since ... since I can remember. I realised with a pang how much pleasure has been missing from my life. They are all three perhaps a year or two younger than myself, and we make an interesting contrast. In many ways they are older and more mature than I, more aware of the ways of the world in general, more travelled, more confident. Quite simply more adult.

Although they are younger than myself, I think of them as women and yet somehow still think of myself as a boy. But in the course of the war I saw and experienced events that have aged me in other ways. I feel it hard to imagine how I could ever again be shocked by people's violence towards one another, or by a wound or an accident, and silly matters like Henry's obsession with bugs – when you have awoken in the night to find a rat sitting on your chest calmly nibbling at a finger it had undoubtedly just removed from a corpse, the prospect of worrying about a few bugs or other insects pales into insignificance.

I did not of course talk about matters like this with the young Danish women, though naturally they were politely curious about my experiences of the war and what had brought me here. They seemed most envious of my spending the summer travelling wherever in the Aegean that fancy takes me, and all agreed that it was wise to take such a break between the discharge of my army service and my resuming my interrupted studies. All said that they wished they had the freedom and finance to do that too, but to me their life here does not seem too awful. They were spending a year in Athens, attending lectures and examining the surrounding archaeological sites, with occasional visits to other sites in places such as Delphi and Epidavros.

It is strange how, in the company of three equally intelligent and beautiful women, one can be instantly attracted to one in particular, for no reason that may easily be analysed. Admittedly, Anna had half-smiled at me the previous day, so was it simply the feeling of knowing that the woman might perhaps be attracted to me? She spoke less than her friends in the course of our meal, yet she was not overshadowed by their personalities. To my mind she is the most striking, yet I could not say why – a look in her pale eyes, a certain look of gentleness in her features? Can people's characters be evident in the set of their face?

I wondered how their lives as students allowed them to afford to eat out at a restaurant every day, even with the modest Greek prices. It seems that their allowance is paid in Denmark, where the cost and the standard of living is high, and when transferred to Greece they are as well-to-do as if they were in employment, with the added advantage that they are living in hostel accommodation, and have a breakfast and evening meal provided at very low cost. I asked why they always dine in the same place when there is such a wide choice in a large city like Athens, but the reason is no more complicated than that one of them, Jutta, has

A.N.A.D.—2

recently taken a liking to the owner's son and is enjoying some harmless flirtation.

By the time that the women told me about this, they had already invited me to the birthday party that was held at their hostel yesterday evening. I suggested that Jutta should invite the manager's son too, and perhaps he and I could arrive together, but the boy was heartbroken because he was working that evening and did not know when he would finish, whether at midnight or even beyond.

The women had their professor's special permission for men to be allowed beyond the doors of the hostel, but as all male visitors had to be out by eleven o'clock the idea was abandoned, although Jutta agreed that perhaps she would see the boy, whose name was Mikalis, when he had his one day off at the end of the week.

The only parties I have ever been to have either been drunken revels in the society of other men at college or very formal occasions, of friends of my parents and so forth (not forgetting the excruciating 'Welcome home the hero' affair for the tenants just before Christmas). And so I was not too sure of what to expect at the hostel, or even what a 'hostel' constituted. There was no question of Dressing, and I cannot help but smile at the memory of my father's quite genuine disbelief when he discovered I would not be packing 'white tie' to take with me to Greece.

He stood there shaking his head and saying 'But you never know, Edward.' Dear father. He is still used to the pre-war days when one took eighteen trunks away just for a house party in the country.

To me, the party in the hostel, with its fun and laughter,

was more civilised in the true sense of the word than any of the stuffy country house dinners I have ever attended.

The presence of Anna, of course, may have had a great deal to do with my way of thinking. Although she was quiet in the restaurant, and not present in the room when I arrived, we were inevitably drawn towards one another and spent much of the evening in earnest conversation. I find the manner in which two people are so drawn together fascinating, as if each were on the end of a piece of invisible thread, slowly being wound closer and closer till they meet face to face.

Of course, the link between Greece and Denmark is obvious. It was Prince William of Denmark, the old man who died only a handful of years ago, who became George I of the Hellenes, when he was chosen king. Like most of the women who were there last night, Anna is blonde – a fact which causes many a local to gape and stare in the street. She is twenty years old, and her parents own a hardware emporium in Copenhagen. There appears to be a strong interest in archaeology in the Scandinavian countries, perhaps because the Scandinavians can trace back their own history a considerable way, to the Vikings and beyond. For some reason, which even she does not understand, Anna picked up this interest at school and having studied classics found herself especially fascinated by the history of ancient Greece – but what student of history could not fail to be interested in a country with such a wealth of sites and material?

Anna is not tall, but is slender and has beautiful clear blue eyes, pale as water. She is the first person I have been attracted to like this since too long ago to remember. The army was – I don't wish to write about that. Enough to say that my emotions were deadened by those years, and feelings towards women can hardly be normal when one has seen the lines of men queuing up for their five minutes 'pleasure' at the red and blue lamps, and then seen the once-beautiful bodies of women and young girls blown apart because life meant they stood in the wrong place at the wrong moment.

Yet if I consider the opposite of that, I do see life can be changed for the good by an equally chance opportunity of being in the right place at the right moment. For chance took me to that restaurant, a million chances brought me to this city at this time, and yet it seemed right to be sitting talking to Anna last night in the hostel's tiny dining room. When the time came for the few men visiting to be turned out onto the streets so that decency could return to the hostel, someone suggested we should go to the restaurant on Constitution Square and reunite Jutta with her Mikalis – by this time everyone knew of the 'romance' in Jutta's life. And although she blushed and said it was late, it did not take a great deal of persuasion for her to join the group (apart from the few sour faces who felt it was time for bed, and were obviously glad to see the back of us).

In the restaurant we indulged ourselves with a brandy, and then were offered a second glass free from the owner, although this was of a noticeably different quality.

As we later walked back to the hostel, I slipped my arm into Anna's, and she looked at me and smiled. She told me that several of the students, herself included, were soon to be making a study trip to Apollo's ancient sanctuary at

Delphi, not too far from Athens, and that if I wanted to see another part of Greece on my travels why not consider making the ferry journey with them in order to have some company?

It would be good if you did, she said. I felt it would be good too, and, simply writing this down I think my mind has been made up, and I will arrange to travel at the same time as her group. Some are a little too quiet and dry for my liking, but there are good people among them. They are apparently taking the ferry to the town of Itea, not over-far from the site of Delphi, and then on by donkey, so the trip in itself might be enjoyable, Today, however, Anna and some others are visiting another site and will be staying there overnight.

22 March

This afternoon I found a dusty bookshop which seemed to contain volumes of all languages, including two shelves crammed with a motley collection of English titles. How a battered copy of *Eric, or Little by Little* finds itself in a shop in the back-streets of Athens, I cannot begin to guess. A former diplomat's reading material, perhaps? I chose instead to spend a few pence on a fairly new edition of Housman's *A Shropshire Lad*, although it is an equally unlikely book to happen across in these circumstances. Perhaps its facility with words will inspire me to improve my own writing.

It is hard to know how good my own writing is. Some

of the poems I have tried do satisfy me, for the most part, but would they satisfy anyone else? Does it matter? I suppose that the important thing is that they record for me the feeling of a particular moment, describe something that happened, or a person I saw. They are, in some ways, a complement to this diary. On these pages I feel I can scribble anything, whatever may occur to me to record, short sentences or whole pages, serious or otherwise. A poem, however, forces me to consider more deeply a particular feeling, to observe a place or person more closely – the exact colours and mood, and so on. The poems shall be

I have forgotten what the poems shall be, for I was interrupted at that point by the arrival of Anna for the evening meal I had invited her to share. It was unnerving to see her and be near her but she was so full of the study trip they had made the previous day that I do not think she noticed. Apparently some unusual pottery shards had been found, and I feel I can share in her excitement. Just as I sensed a link with the past when I was walking in and about the site of the Acropolis, so can I imagine the thrill an archaeologist must feel when unearthing an object that has lain under the earth for thousands of years, an object actually held and used by a man or woman of the ancient world. Anna's eyes sparkled with joy as she told me of the finds. How good it was to see someone so full of the pleasures of being alive. Lord knows how appreciative I am of that fact.

We dined at a table on the pavement on a street corner, at a small place where I had eaten lunch one day when I first arrived. The place is close to Anna's hostel and specialises in a variety of fish. For a nation almost surrounded by coast line, one of whose principal activities is fishing, the catch is remarkably expensive to eat. Nevertheless, we sat and watched the people at the other tables, and the passers-by. Anna shares my curiosity about passers-by, and my interest in conjecturing who they are, what they are doing and where they are going. There was a middle-aged man and a young woman at one table along from us – father and daughter, man and wife, friends, lovers?

Yet another pleasure I am discovering in being here is the way in which a meal will last for the whole of an evening. In Greece this is no doubt partly attributable to the slowness of the service, and the way in which the waiter will stop to talk to his regular customers while others are clamouring for wine, food or more bread. With good company and a bottle of wine, in what better way could an evening imaginably be spent?

I cannot imagine a better companion than Anna at this moment. There have been times when I could never imagine a woman taking an interest in me again. One ached so hard – between bouts of numbness – for a hot bath, clean clothes and the company of a gentle sweet-smelling woman. Yet the possibility seemed so far removed from life that it was hard to believe that it might actually happen. We were all at it were trapped in the depths of winter while trying to imagine not merely next summer but three summers hence.

It is not yet summer, but this evening I luxuriated in the company of a beautiful sweet-smelling woman, herself surely freshly bathed. I treasured every moment of the meal we ate. Anna encouraged me in my experimentation with local food by suggesting that I try squid, my only experience of that creature until now being the battle of the giant squids in the book *Twenty Thousand Leagues under the Sea*.

I rather imagined that a large earthenware plate would arrive containing one giant tentacle, which would hang over each side. In fact, the pieces of fish (or is it meat?) were small, cooked beautifully in olive oil to render them crisp, and tasted like a slightly tough variety of chicken. I enjoyed it immensely, and wondered to Anna how our fathers might react if presented with such a dish. I cannot decide which mine would find more upsetting, the prospect of the meal itself or the difficulty in deciding upon a suitable wine! I must remember to send him a report of my visit to the Acropolis.

For us, however, there proved to be no difficulty in deciding on a wine. The retsina has become my regular drink, and I feel when I swallow a glass of it that I am downing a draught of pure ancient Greece.

After the meal we walked part of the way towards Anna's hostel, and stopped for a final glass of Metaxa in a bar nearby. Perhaps it was the combination of retsina and brandy that made me bold, but as we set off on the final part of our stroll I placed my arm firmly around her waist, much relieved to see the way in which she looked at me and smiled, then pressed closer to me as we walked.

At the reception to the hostel is customarily positioned a rather severe-looking Danish woman, with hair stiffly scraped back, whose responsibility it is to check all the students in and out each evening, and to lock the doors and scrutinise visitors. Not wishing to be scrutinised too closely as we said our goodnights, we lingered a moment in an adjacent doorway, unobserved in the darkness. I had already told Anna that I would like to travel to Delphi when she left with the others in little over a week, and, as we were parting, she told me softly how pleased she was that I would be there too.

She lifted her face to me and I kissed her gently on the forehead, but then she lifted her face in more obvious fashion and I pressed my lips against her own warm, wet and beautifully soft ones. I found myself almost overwhelmed at holding her and breathing in the sweet scent of her. Though my hand was only holding her in the small of the back, I could not help but be aware of the firmness of her slender body beneath and its arousing effect on me. She is the first woman I have ever kissed in this manner, discounting a few clumsy attempts in my youth, such as that with Agnes, when noses always seemed to get in the way.

I was left in a turmoil of emotion, for I fear that Anna was aware of my arousal too, and with only a few brief words to arrange for a meeting tomorrow, she skipped quickly away and into the protective confines of her hostel. I stopped to take another brandy along the way, and returned to the hotel rather befuddled from drink and a confusion of feelings, hoping I had not offended her.

24 March

Though my intention has been to record day by day, if

possible, the events of my trip, those good intentions are not always realised. There are certain days, such as yesterday, which it might be better to avoid or which are not worth recording in excessive detail. I cannot imagine wanting to look back and remember yesterday in years to come.

I awoke with a raging headache, as if my brain was being knocked down and rebuilt to a more modern design. It was certainly of little use to me in its original form, and I was scarcely able to put two words together (in any language) for much of the morning. A new guest had joined Henry and myself at our breakfast table and I was pleased that they were able to divert each other while I concentrated on my dry bread and my coffee without milk.

The new man, Kurt, is a hearty Austrian walker whose conversation is punctuated with laughs as solid as the thighs that bulge out of his incongruous lederhosen. With thighs of that magnitude, I can imagine him walking the length and troubled breadth of Europe, and to judge from his boasting he has already seen as much as there is to see. Listening to him, one might think that the war was merely fought to provide an unwarranted intrusion into his walking activities, but now that it is past he is determined to resume striding out in whichever direction he happens to be facing. He condescended to travel to Athens by train, but now that he is here he is looking forward to walking as much as is possible of the apparently lovely Greek countryside. An enviable idea, but I shall also be seeing at least a glimpse of it. Anna has suggested that we take a picnic at the weekend, and go out of Athens on the morning train to a small village that she knows, and return by the train in the evening.

I was delighted at this idea, which Anna suggested yesterday evening, particularly after my anxieties of the night before. It seems that I need not have been worried that Anna would be offended by the all too evident signs of my passion, for she was plainly delighted to see me again and we passed a pleasant evening, followed by an even more exquisite time kissing, my hand cupping the cloth that covered her breast in the darkness of the doorway near the hostel.

I was mildly surprised (although pleased) to hear her say that it was a pity I could not come into the hostel with her, as we would be much more comfortable inside. These were inviting words which I cannot imagine ever coming from the lips of an English woman, unless, perhaps, in a hot and romantic climate; though it is still difficult to imagine such openness. And the Nordic races are said to be cool and lacking in passion!

Perhaps I am misunderstanding Anna's invitation, and she merely meant that it would be pleasant to sit and kiss awhile in the privacy of her room, but I was sure I detected there a hint of intimacy. Tonight I wondered if I should suggest that we return to my own room, but perhaps that might be too bold a remark. And besides, there is the question of access to the room. Although we have our own keys and need not surrender them at the desk each time we go in and out, how would Anna escape the eagle eye of the manager, Mr Kalamatis, or his night porter, Dimitrios?

I have now discovered that my hotel is not far distant from a small red-light quarter, and that some of the other hotels in this area have a bad reputation. Mr Kalamatis is proud of the standards of his hotel (Henry's bugs notwithstanding), and I cannot imagine him in any way approving of a male guest taking a female visitor to his room late at night.

I wish I had more experience with women, indeed I wish I had *some* experience! There were many chances to take women in the army, but paying to be 44th in line for some haggard whore had no appeal for me. There were other ordinary women about too, of course, yet I never met one whom I might have felt passionate towards – or perhaps I chose not to, as my emotional life was much deadened during those events abroad. Visits home on leave merely represented a false peace – I knew what I was soon to be returning to. Mother did try to lighten my homecomings by introducing me to likely candidates, daughters of friends and so on, but her capacity for choosing the most wholly unsuitable partner was for me unbounded. I think she was worried at what might have been happening to me under the influence of all those 'common' soldiers as she saw them, although having survived school and its attendant temptations, she need not have worried in that respect.

Now I am the one with the worries. I wish I could guess what Anna expected of me. I admit that uncertainty does add excitement to our relationship but how is one to know what a woman expects of a relationship? Does she feel the same desires?

Perhaps I should not worry quite so much, and let events take care of themselves. My mind drifts to all manner of thoughts late at night by the low lamplight of this room, listening to the shouts in the streets below. Then there is the other question.

25 March

I returned to the dingy bookshop this morning and bought for myself an old English-Greek dictionary, and also a small grammar, and studied them both in a café while I was still in the busy market quarter near the foot of the Acropolis. I felt that I would be more likely to find what I needed in this area of the city, than in the more fashionable shops nearer the centre; although neither of the books were of any help to me.

There *must* be a Greek word for contraceptive! What it is, however, the dictionary's compilers have chosen not to reveal. I admit that it is not a word there will be much call for in translating the ancient language of Sophocles, or studying Pythagoras, but surely in these times the compilers of modern dictionaries must see that the word has a right to exist.

After perusing all the possibilities, the closest I could get was 'conception', and several words beginning with 'contra-', but quite how one combined the two, and what the resulting meaning would be, I was at a loss to tell. Undoubtedly, using the wrong word could cause anything from howls of laughter to a diplomatic incident. There was also the question of where to try to obtain such unmentionable objects. Using my small ability to read the alphabet, I can discern that some shops are the equivalent of 'apothecary', although I hope sincerely that they are somewhat more up-to-date than their name might suggest. What devilish device one might receive in such an establishment is too horrific to contemplate. A pig's bladder if one were very lucky.

My major concern was what to ask for. My invented word of 'contra-conception' seemed to be less likely to yield results the more I considered it, and it would take weeks of studying Greek grammar before I would be able to construct a phrase. I decided I would make an attempt at the word 'contra-conception', and hang the consequences. I constructed my sentence, which was basic in the extreme, 'I want contra-conception'. I then changed my mind, as the result would undoubtedly be even more ludicrous in Greek than it was in English, with the added drawback that it might mean something totally different in translation if, indeed, it meant anything at all.

However, the thought of Anna, a picnic in a secluded spot, or a night together somehow, perhaps in Delphi, all prompted me to decide that no matter how ridiculous and embarrassing the outcome might be, I had to at least make an attempt to buy what I needed. If only I had thought to make such purchases in England!

I paid for the two small coffees and the two ouzos that I had finished while making my deliberations, and set off purposefully towards an 'apothecary' whose sign I could see in a narrow side street facing the café. I quickly decided to look first into the window and then perhaps into the shop. What I discovered in the window was none too encouraging, as the display seemed not to have been changed for at least fifty years. The writing on the packaging of the items had faded in the light to an almost uniform pale yellow, like a weak tea. I would not have been able to tell what the items were in any case, and in some instances I was relieved that I did not know. Some small boxes appeared to house devices of a most dubious nature, while a cat basking in a shaft of sunlight can have done little for the scent of the perfume samples over which it was lazily flicking its tail.

Of the interior of the shop I could see nothing, but deciding that I had nothing to lose by attempting my request I went inside. Sitting deep in the shadows I could see a man who looked as if he might have been present when they originally built the Acropolis, so old and wizened did he appear. He was clacking one of the sets of beads that I frequently see Greek men carrying and idly flicking in their hands. These help them disperse all their worries. Certainly a less worried man I could not imagine, and I wished vehemently that I too possessed a set of beads at that moment.

The man greeted me with an almost imperceptible nod, and I stammered my request for some contra-conception. He repeated the last word with a slight lift of the eyebrows, which I understood to mean that I was probably along the right lines, so I nodded.

Without rising from his chair, he propelled himself along behind the counter, and emerged to inspect the shelves along the other side of the shop. I could see that his chair was on small wheels, but could not decide whether the man was crippled in some way or merely being lazy. He still did not stand, but spying what he was seeking, turned to take a long pole from the counter and reached up with this to one of the higher shelves. On the end of this pole were two finger-like pincers, and by tugging on two strings he was able to use these like a pair of pliers and close them around the package he wanted to reach. He lifted this down, spun around in his chair and presented me with the packet.

I was so surprised at all this that I had long since lost my initial embarrassment and merely accepted the package. I took some coins from my pocket and looked at him quizzically. He said something which I could not understand (I must start to study my numbers), so I gestured to him to write it down, whereupon he propelled himself by his feet along the front of the counter, and almost knocked me over in the process. He scribbled '25' on a scrap of paper with a scrap of pencil and, although it seemed expensive, I hurriedly paid him and left.

By now it was almost time to meet Anna and her friends for lunch, and I decided it would be safest if I returned my acquisitions to my hotel room.

After lunch, which was the usual pleasant affair full of laughter, I returned to my room to inspect my purchase, and opened the mysterious box. Inside was a small jar, which appeared to be full of ointment. Its smell was quite pleasant, but that was hardly compensation for the fact that it was obviously not meant to serve the purpose for which I had bought it. I decided that all I could do was return it to the shop, though what I would say when I got there was not immediately clear to me.

26 March

What a saga my story of yesterday is turning into! When I walked into the shop in the hope of exchanging my ointment for something more suitable, and approached the man, I realised to my surprise that he was now a woman, or rather that an equally ancient woman was occupying the place where he had been sitting the previous day. Before she could fly out at me on the chair I turned tail. '*Pardon*', I muttered in French, which I am well aware was a useless thing to say but, not knowing the Greek word for 'Sorry', uttering it in French rather than English seemed for some strange reason to be slightly preferable.

These days, when in doubt I retreat to the nearest café to drink an ouzo while I organise my thoughts which, at that moment, were indeed well and truly jumbled. I had a jar of ointment which I did not want, I needed something intimate which I did not know how to ask for, and I might or might not be on the verge of losing my innocence to a Danish archaeologist. If I were not on the verge, then all this activity was fruitless. But how was I to know whether I was or was not until the moment itself dawned?

I can hardly ask Anna what her intentions are towards me, although I am certainly aware what my intentions now are towards her, after the late-night kisses and embraces we have been exchanging.

As I sipped at my ouzo, I reflected that I could try visiting another 'apothecary' and repeating my request, but I might only then find myself in possession of two jars of this mysterious and costly ointment. I could hardly explain to father why I needed an additional remittance, for what I needed is not generally recognised as part of the amateur classical scholar's equipment. I searched again through my dictionary and decided that an alternative description of what I wanted might help, and after a little thought I decided that the words 'birth' and 'prevention' might, if strung together, have approximately the same meaning in Greek as they do in English.

After a short while, I saw the old woman leaving the apothecary, and reasoning that they would not be likely to leave the shop unattended I walked over again to see if the man had resumed his place behind the counter, which indeed he had. He greeted me with the same imperceptible nod. I showed him the jar he had sold me and emphatically said *Ochi*, meaning 'No' – one of the handful of Greek words and phrases of which I am reasonably sure. I tried again with 'contra-conception', and the man equally emphatically pointed to the jar and said *Neh, neh*, which (contrary to all expectation) is the Greek for 'Yes'.

I shook my head.

It may have been what I asked for, but was definitely not what I wanted. I tried again with my 'birth prevention' phrase, and a slight light dawned in his eyes. He laughed and punched my hip from his seat in the chair, and made a mime around his private parts which could only mean that he emphatically did understand my request this time. Genuine tears came into his eyes as he spoke to himself, and I could only nod and smile and pretend to share in the joke.

Eventually the old man picked up his long wooden pole and returned the jar in its box to the shelf, taking instead another box from a different shelf. This he handed to me, opening it up to show me that what I wanted was indeed inside. I quickly closed the box as another customer came into the shop but to little avail, as the whole episode was recounted amid mutual laughter and back-slapping, while the smile on my face became even more frozen.

Anxious to leave, I took money from my pocket, but the shopkeeper waved it away, reached into a drawer and returned to me the 25 drachmas I had spent there the day before. It needed no dictionary or grammar to translate what he was saying as he forced the money into my hand: take it, take it, it's worth it for the laughs alone.

When his wife appeared in the doorway and the old man began his story anew, I thanked him and hastily left. I have vowed to try to avoid that quarter of Athens from now on. Though I have not the slightest idea what the confusion was about, I am sure the story will have spread like wildfire through the shops and to my favoured tavern nearby. The most baffling thing about the whole embarrassing affair is that it was all done for the most romantic notions of love. What a rum business it all is.

29 March

Well – how do I begin, now the weekend is past?

Anna had promised to organise our food for the picnic, leaving me to bring along the wine, water and a rug on which to sit. On Friday, I went out and bought everything, and also, to carry them, a tough leather shoulder-bag from a busy workshop in the old part of the city. What a strong, beautiful smell new leather has, powerful as a furnace. I was joined for Saturday breakfast at the hotel by a young couple from France, but from Languedoc in the south, where I had not been. They have moved in to the small room vacated by Henry two days ago, but as they made no complaint about bites in the night I can only assume that the bugs left with Henry! I suppose he was amusing to have about, in his own way; although the conversation at breakfast has now improved immeasurably!

As we'd agreed, I met Anna at the station and was happy to leave the task of buying the tickets to her. After my recent foray into mastering the Greek language, who knows where we might have found ourselves? My embarrassment at the incidents in the apothecary's has worn off somewhat, and I can laugh a little at it: I may as well, since everyone else appeared to be doing so. It is tiresome not to be able to share the events with Anna. Part of my pleasure in being with her and, I trust, hers in being with me, is to share the incidents of the day. A pleasure shared is undoubtedly a pleasure doubled. Have I just invented a mathematical aphorism?

With Anna's fair looks and our picnic basket we were the objects of intense curiosity on the journey. The dusty carriage was filled with people, all of whom seemed to have an insatiable appetite for personal detail – who are you, where are you from, where are you going, are you married, what are your jobs; and more difficult, what do you think of the situation in Greece? The list is endless. Yet there was no sense of prying – the questioning was too open for that.

Four of the women in the carriage wore the black of widow's weeds, and I noticed that they crossed themselves at intervals. Anna explained that this was as we passed a church, and I began to watch out for these through the windows, but it seems that the women's eyesight was infinitely better than my own as there would be a flurry of cross-making while all I could see from the window was coarse green grass and a few thin goats. Perhaps the churches were beyond the hills, but in that case where would one draw the line? Over the next hill? Two miles away? It was noticeable that the men did not join in this devotion, apart from one small chap in the corner (about one-third the size of his wife) who occasionally flapped his hands across his ribs, in a vague manner.

By the time we descended from the train, after about an hour's worth of rattling journey from the station in Athens, we were laden with presents given by people in the carriage, wishing us well on our day out. The thin man and his wife wrapped us some cheese in a page from their newspaper, another woman in black gave us two tomatoes huge as watermelons, another ripped a cucumber in half, while someone else cut us two slabs of bread which I felt, if nothing else, we could always use to sit on. But their generosity was overwhelming.

As we walked away from the station, which appeared to be in the middle of nowhere, although Anna assured me it served one busy village lying just behind the hill and other smaller villages scattered around, we talked of this generosity of spirit. I had only, as yet, encountered this in small ways, a cigarette offered by a stranger in a café, the shopkeeper refusing payment for one of my purchases, a free brandy one evening, but Anna insisted that the gifts on the train were typical of the larger kindnesses that simple people show to each other, and, more particularly, to strangers.

It seems that there is a word in the Greek language which

Anna pronounced *Zenos*, which means both a stranger and guest. The two concepts are inseparable, which fascinates me. Moreover, it shows that a knowledge of a foreign language does not serve only to enable you to speak in that language, but also to understand something of the people on a deeper level. The Greeks have one word for stranger/guest. We separate the two. So what do Greeks do when they learn English, forget their own philosophy of treating the stranger as a guest, and try to decide which of the two a person is?

This subject occupied us until we left the main track and walked up through the dry soil of an olive grove towards the peak of a small hill. There, surrounded by the clanking of the bells of a herd of goats that wandered curiously around us, we set down our blanket and rested. The surroundings were so peaceful, the view so beautiful, that if I were a painter I would have had to capture the moment for ever on canvas. As it is, I have to content myself with words.

It seemed the easiest thing in the world, at that moment, to lean across and kiss Anna, who was now lying on her back with eyes closed absorbing the warmth of the sun. As my head moved over hers and put her face in shadow, she opened her eyes, and, not by moving but by merely thinking it, beckoned me down. It was as if my face mixed into hers and was absorbed by it, our mouths joined, and my lips moved over hers, hers over mine. I could feel the warmth of the sun on the back of my head, and her hand ruffling and stroking my hair as our mouths moved gently in a mesmerising motion. I was surprised when Anna used her tongue to kiss, gently but firmly forcing it between my open lips and into my mouth – surprised but thrilled with the hot wet feel of it, its muscular softness.

It was then that Anna opened her blue eyes again to gaze into mine, and then her gaze shifted over my shoulder and suddenly she snorted and laughed as she pulled her mouth away.

'Don't move,' she said, 'but turn your head round slowly.'

This I did, and found myself gazing into the intent face of a goat no more than two feet away from me. It had a puzzled look in its eyes, a straggly grey beard, and about six inches of newspaper dangling from its mouth. The paper flicked from one side to the other as the goat made a speculative chew, then back to the other as it repeated the process, until finally the paper disappeared completely with a kind of slurping sound. When we made no move, the goat bent its head and helped itself to another piece. It evidently preferred the wrapping to the cheese, a preference we were quite able to understand when we later sampled the cheese.

Our romantic interlude had been interrupted for the time being, so we settled down to eat our picnic while we still had some of it left. I made what I thought a witty remark about 'playing the giddy goat', and spent five minutes trying to explain to Anna exactly what a giddy goat is – evidently the Danish language lacks the equivalent phrase.

While we set to our meal of cold meat and salad, and downed the delicious if slightly warm wine, the goat finished the newspaper and looked greedily at the very blanket we sat on. Upon attempting to turn the looks into action I chased it off and the goat stood at a distance of about ten yards, edging forward by a matter of a few inches each time we looked away. After several minutes it would once again be standing, as if by magic, a couple of feet from the blanket. Whereupon I would do my duty and shoo it away once again. Its persistence eventually earned it an apple. Our attempts to persuade it to eat the cheese were a spectacular failure, even though what rendered it unappetising to us should have had the goat licking its lips in anticipation, for its softness had absorbed much of the newsprint from the paper and the cheese was more readable than edible.

For a while in the afternoon we were joined by a young Greek boy, whom I suppose I could romanticize with the description of 'goatherd', though he was just an ordinary village boy out after school to check the goats for his father. His round brown face was wreathed in shy smiles as he looked up at us through his lashes when answering our questions. We offered him an apple and accepted drinks from his water bottle in return. The goatskin bottle was slung over his shoulder on a leather strap, just as it might have been 3,000 years ago.

I pause now for a while to eat by myself (Anna has an engagement), and almost feel that I am marking time till we leave for Delphi, where we should have better opportunity to be together again.

We decided to walk with the young Greek boy into the nearby village to take a look before catching our train back to Athens. While Anna and I were agreeing this, the boy, Stelios, asked if he could ride in our motor-car before we left, and when we explained that we had no such car but had arrived on the train and would return that way he told us that there was no train now until Sunday.

'But they told me in Athens there was a train at six o'clock,' Anna insisted.

'*Exi ora*,' she said to Stelios.

'*Exi ora*?' His reply was not quite so simple to my ear, but Anna translated it as 'Yes, but not on Saturdays.' Anna did not look too perturbed, and I think I almost suspect that she knew there would be no train.

'We can find somewhere to stay in the village,' she said, 'if you do not mind.'

Anna and the boy exchanged words, then he ran away in furious speed towards the village.

'He said we could stay in his grandmother's empty room. Travellers have stayed there before. You do not mind to share a room?'

I smiled and said I did not!

Anna smiled too. 'Good,' she said. Anna had rings on her right hand which she moved to the third finger of her left hand, explaining that, so as not to risk offending the grandmother or anyone else, we were now married.

Stelios was soon back, breathless, with the news that his grandmother was making the room ready, and we were to go to the café to give her a little more time. Would ten drachmae be too much to pay, his grandmother wanted to know. I thought of the cost of my hotel room and was sure that Stelios must have made a mistake with the price, or that we were to be put into some stable with a hole in the roof. Anna assured me that this was quite a normal price to pay, as rooms in village houses were very cheap indeed, and the students often stayed in these when visiting sites in more out

A.N.A.D.—3

of the way places. They were usually clean too, she said, although washing and lavatory facilities often apparently left much to be desired. And I told Anna that I thought for one night I could happily bear that.

I shall continue this entry later this afternoon. My hand is about to stiffen from all this writing, and I intend to get down every moment of this weekend.

The village itself was tiny, little more than a rough main street with side streets leading away into nothing. We sat at the café, which also served as taverna, shop and even, in one corner, a butcher's. As the men sat and stared at us, I tried not to look too hard at the lumps of all-too-bloody meat that were being hacked at from time to time. The women who were coming to buy were certainly getting the freshest of cuts – at least the owner had the decency to wear a different apron when butchering from when he was waiting at table.

We bought a glass filled with fresh orange mixed with honey for Stelios, and he sat beside us with great pride, the friend of the first foreign visitors of the year. His shyness with us when we met him alone on the hill was no longer evident now we were back in his village. The owner of the café introduced himself to us as Jorgos, and came to sit with us when he was not busy, which was much of the time. His wife attended the shop, but remained in the shadows behind the counter, a thin ghostly figure whose eyes twinkled out of the gloom. Naturally enough, we were figures of great curiosity, for Jorgos told us that visitors were few and far between, though the village was getting busier now that the business of war was over. Last summer maybe five or six people had stayed in the village overnight and dined at his restaurant (as he proudly described it) and perhaps the same number again or more would stop for a time or make the rattling train journey out from Athens.

Jorgos made Athens sound like a distant country, instead of a shortish train journey away. This summer would be even better – already they had two visitors and it was not yet even Easter.

From time to time, Stelios would race off to see if his grandmother had made ready the room; although we were in no hurry to move. Indeed, it would have been difficult to move, for we were soon hemmed in, as it seemed, by much of the village's male population. It was noticeable that the women would not sit at the tables as they were passing through to buy meat or something from the shop. They would nod to us and say hello (Anna explained the various greetings), but the café was evidently a male preserve – Greece is still very much a country of men, although the women maintain a strong background presence. Already the figure of Stelios's grandmother has taken on quite a strong memory in my mind. The grandfather, presumably, is dead although even if he were not I imagine that the arrangements for the room, or for anything to do with the home, would have been the grandmother's affair.

We answered the inevitable questions – or rather Anna did, translating for me, which gave us a little time to think as she turned to me with an almost imperceptible smile in her eyes and asked where we lived, how long we had been married, did we not have children, and so forth. In fact it was remarkably easy to devise a life for us, of a meeting on a visit to England by Anna soon after the war, a marriage shortly afterwards (greeted with a shout equivalent to 'Bravo!' by the men, who evidently cherished some romance in their souls), her final year of studies here, myself coming to stay with her before resuming my own studies when we returned to England at the end of the summer. With the romance of the story and the respect these untutored men have for education, we were very soon the heroes of the hour, being noisily wished well and toasted every few minutes.

By now Stelios had returned with the news that at last we could inspect his grandmother's room, so we followed him to the house, leaving behind us firm promises that we would eat in the café that evening.

Stelios's grandmother was waiting for us in the doorway of the house, a bony stooped woman of great but indeterminate age and even greater warmth. She led us around the outside of her house to the room at the back, which had a separate doorway suggesting that it was originally used for animals. There was no sign of them now, for the walls were freshly whited and the stone floor was clean, with a grey-white sheepskin rug by the wooden bed. The old woman heaved the rug onto the bed and nodded, to ensure that we understood this was to be used to keep us warm if necessary.

Aside from the bed, which was obviously ancient, the room had two old tables, one holding a white and yellow washbasin in which was standing a matching jug of cold water, the other table by the bed with a matchbox, a stub of candle and a small spray of red and yellow flowers in a battered tin cup. The contrast between the delicate petals and the chipped, rough rusting metal was very moving, and when I picked up the flowers and smelled them with Anna, the grandmother smiled a gap-toothed smile. No bouquet in a porcelain vase could have given us more pleasure at that moment than our own enamel cup of flowers.

A bath of some kind would have been welcome, but it seemed that this was not on offer so we contented ourselves with washing our faces and hands in the basin of cold water, emptying it afterwards over the roots of the skeletal vine that was waiting for summer in the old woman's garden.

We rested awhile and compared our observations of the village and its people. I had noticed especially the shabbiness of the clothing, even more marked there than in the poor quarters of Athens where it is noticeable enough. Every second or third man that you see in the city will have the elbow missing from his jacket and his jumper poking through, or his shirt visible through a hole in the jumper, or holes in the knees (or worse places) of the trousers. Yet they carry themselves with great dignity, as did the men in this village, whose clothes were thin and faces unshaven. But as with the rusty tin can that held our flowers, I would rather have the company of the men with whom we ate that evening than attend the finest of my family's dinner parties. The food was simple but delicious – a cut of lamb still on the bone with a kind of vegetable stew, and the talk and drink both flowed freely and could undoubtedly have gone on into the night, but Anna told them we were tired from an early start and much walking, and we returned to our room feeling warm and comfortable.

I bumped around in the dark till I was able to locate and light the candle. When I had done so the flame suffused the room with a rich golden glow which reflected my feelings. I walked slowly towards Anna and as she raised her face to mine, we kissed. At first very gently, our lips just touching and nibbling, until passion took hold and I pushed my tongue between Anna's lips, her mouth opening to take it, pressing it with her own tongue, then pushing it and thrusting her tongue into my mouth.

Then Anna pulled away and pushed me back, so that I was sitting on the edge of the bed. 'Stay there,' she instructed me. In the light of the candle she began slowly to undress, enjoying me watching her, not knowing that it would be the first time I had seen a woman naked. My gut tightened and my heart pounded at the thought. She removed first her shoes, then her short white ankle socks, and dropped them onto the thick grey rug. She was wearing a long dress of pale blue that buttoned at the front, and she began to undo this slowly, looking at me and smiling as she prised the buttons apart, peeling the dress from her, and letting it fall so that it fell round her feet like a fragment of crumpled sky.

She stepped out of this and lifted her thin white underskirt, pulling it up and over her head so that I could see her breasts, as she stood before me in only a pair of white pants. She stood still for a moment while I looked, fixated by the beauty of her small, shapely breasts, which were tipped with tiny erect buds of pink. Then turning her back to me she took down her pants, bending as she pulled them over her feet, and I felt that my chest would burst with the surge of pleasure that went through me at the sight of the smooth lines of her back, her bottom and her legs. Then she stood full height again and turned to face me, arms by her side, her head tilted at an angle. She smiled and asked, 'You like?'

'Yes, I like,' I told her. I kept my eyes on her face at first, then let them linger over her perfect shoulders and breasts, finally lowering them to gaze at her body hair, the flimsiest of honeyed curls, matching the honeyed look of her skin coloured darker by the flickering light of the candle. Her body cast a flowing shadow against the walls of the room. I was still sitting on the edge of the bed and I beckoned her to me, opening my legs to let her approach me. I wrapped my arms round her and pressed my face against her stomach, then ran my hands over her back, her hips, and cupped her bottom. I moved my fingers down to caress her thighs, then pushed them up and between the tops of her legs till the tips met a warmer skin, wet and downy to the touch.

Anna sucked in her breath and uttered a low groan as I touched her there. She tugged at the buttons on my shirt, and together we pulled off my clothes and took the cover off the bed till we knelt there naked and facing each other on the cool white sheet. I did not truly know what arousal meant until that night, as I looked at Anna and wanted to touch or taste every part of her, to kiss her and be inside her, wrapped together as one.

She reached out to take me in her hand, and squeezed me gently so that the pleasure swept through every part of me. Still kneeling and facing me, she moved her legs apart, and I reached forward and fingered her too, as she was touching me, and as I gently stroked the moist lips between her legs, she moved her hand slowly up and down my shaft, easing the skin back and forth, grasping its thickness and building the pleasure inside me. Soft moans and sudden breaths came from her, and I hesitantly pushed a finger further inside her – it went in and up into her, in the warm wet passage that gripped and released me, gripped and released, then to my surprise she put her hand on my wrist, guided her own fingers across the backs of mine, and manoeuvred the finger that was in her till it rested on a bud just inside her swollen lips, hidden by the tiniest folds of skin.

'There,' she said, 'touch me there,' and I touched her, moving my finger back and forth, discovering what pleased her, and 'More,' she said, and 'More,' till after a moment she let go of me, and leaned away.

'Wait,' she insisted, reaching for her bag that was lying by the bed.

'You must wear this,' she said, and from a small paper packet produced the very object that had caused me such embarrassment to try to buy. She too had thought of that, and she held me while I pushed on the sheath then she lay down and parted her knees, lifted one leg and pulled me towards her with the foot, and I lay over her and thrust myself into her, with a delicious and indescribable feeling of pleasure. Soon I felt myself ready to burst inside her, wanting to reach her very heart, and with Anna breathing 'Yes, yes' in my ear I spurted wildly, again and again, in the most magical moment I have ever experienced in my life.

Anna was panting hotly, insisting 'Go on, go on,' and although her pleasure seemed to be turning slowly to pain

I continued to push for as long as I was able until at last she emitted a sound that was a scream, a squeal, a strangled gasp, and held me tightly to her as she lay in silence for a time, trembling and whimpering.

We whispered gentle words to each other, then I removed the sheath, blew out the candle, and we drifted warmly into sleep in each other's arms – as if none of the ills of the world could ever touch us. This is my first experience of being with a woman, and I cannot imagine that other times can possibly be as good. It was as if years of waiting had accumulated to increase the pleasure immeasurably. Words are unable to capture the true feelings, the warmth, the wonderment, but they do at least record it honestly, for better or worse.

30 March

After the events of the weekend, I am looking forward with even greater pleasure to the time in Delphi. Anna informs me that the student accommodation will be in rooms in the nearby village, and that she has put her name down for a single room, although normally she would prefer to share with a friend. It seems that there is little chance that we will be able to take a room together, since we could not possibly hope to keep this a secret for very long. Although many of the students are open and friendly and would, I imagine, turn a blind eye to a romantic involvement, there are others who seem to pursue pleasure with a religious fervour, to stamp it out.

The professor who is to accompany the trip, amusingly enough called Professor Andersen, would probably not be amused to discover that one of his students was sharing a room with an Englishman. He is, after all, responsible for both physical and moral welfare of those students in his charge, and should anything untoward happen, might well lose his position. Indeed the professors here have a difficult job, as many of the female students are extremely attractive, and being foreign and single quite naturally arouse great interest in the young Greek men. The Greeks, too, are a good-looking race, many of the younger men having quite striking features, thin and angular (in contrast to the shape they tend to assume when older), while the Greek women have more rounded faces, a dark-eyed olive-skinned beauty.

Nevertheless, if I also find myself a single room, with some degree of privacy, then Anna and I can look forward to more nights like the one that we have just shared. I am sure that there will be a choice of accommodation at this time of the year.

At the moment all my thoughts seem to turn either back to the weekend, or forward to Delphi, and this makes it somewhat hard to live in the present. If it were not for the rules of the hostel, Anna and I could perhaps take a hotel room somewhere for a few days, but the students have to be checked in and out, and watchful eyes note any mysterious disappearances, or non-appearances. And the students risk being sent home if their behaviour is in any way lacking. But an interesting thought has just occurred to me inspired, no doubt, by the fact that the trip to Delphi seems such a long time hence (we go there on Friday, and today is only Monday). I shall suggest it to Anna when we eat together tonight.

The rest of today I intend to spend studying my Greek grammar, in the hope that I can knock at least a smattering of this language into me. I must also write home, as I haven't yet answered father's last letter, and if I go to the Post Office to check I am sure there will be another from mother awaiting me.

31 March

I managed to get a letter off to father yesterday and when I visited the *poste restante* this morning, as I expected, there was indeed a letter from mother for me. Why cannot they combine their letters? It is not that their separate letters repeat each other's news and information, and a joint letter would therefore be shorter – in that respect, in fact, they seem to lead completely different lives. Mother's letter is full of news of Aunt Belinda, Uncle Dickie, and other relatives of whom I am sure I have never heard. I will ask her to draw me a family tree one day, so that these far-flung and very distant cousins who are having babies or dying or running away with the servants will all make sense to me. Mother also writes about dinner parties and events in the village. 'Those dear people,' I can just hear her saying.

Father, on the other hand, tells me of his trips to London,

of his various business interests, of increased dividends on his stocks and what his business partners are up to. I try to maintain an interest in this, but most of it seems supremely irrelevant to me in my present situation. I am grateful, however, that he does take the trouble to write, which many a father I am sure would not. And it is only natural that he wants me to maintain an interest in his various businesses. He is quite proud of my taking up a university place, but I know that beneath it all he still expects me to get this classical education over and done with and settle down to earning my living (although what use an English degree will be in the running of factories I am not sure).

I suggested my plan to Anna last night, which was that we should go today to a hotel somewhere close by and take a room together, pretending to be man and wife, and that perhaps after returning to the hostel in the evening she might be able to find a back way out, through a window or something similar, and then I would meet her and we would be able to spend the night together at the hotel. She could then go straight to her lecture or workings in the morning. She said, simply, that the last student who tried to do that is now back in Denmark, having suffered the indignity of being sent down. Apparently there is always someone to notice your absence, either another student in the dormitory, or one of the staff at the communal breakfast the next morning. So that was the end of my inspired idea. But, it is now another day closer to Friday – and might we not possibly be together on Friday evening? I shall write back to mother at once and tell her how I am looking forward to my visit to Delphi.

1 April

Last night there was at least a hint of the pleasures to come – as we said our goodnights in the dark doorway near to the hostel entrance, I slid my hand gently up to Anna's breast, and felt its soft contours, that wonderful yielding feeling – her breast is the softest skin I have ever felt, delicate and tender in the way it gives and moves – and the miraculous way in which the harder skin of the tip will expand with pleasure, nuzzling into your palm. Even through the layers of her clothing I could feel her nipple straining and budding to the touch. Anna knows about the scar on the inside of my right thigh, her fingers touched it inquisitively that night in the village, but she has not asked me about it and I have not told her.

Bringing my thoughts back to daytime, this morning I told the hotel manager that I would be leaving on Friday, to go to Delphi, and he immediately informed me that he has a cousin there with rooms to rent and I must seek out the cousin as soon as I arrive: Yanni Kalamatis. He wrote the name and address for me on a piece of paper, and said that if I showed this to anyone in the town they would know who it was and be able to direct me. I promised I would try, but if this Mr Kalamatis has the same eagle eye as his cousin here then I do not think that taking a room with him will lead to the delights that Anna and I have in mind.

This morning I made a return to the Acropolis, wanting to be sure of seeing it at least once more before I moved. I do intend to visit Athens again before returning home to

England, but who knows what may occur? Illness, disaster, change of circumstances, all can happen at any moment. The country is not politically as calm as it seems outwardly, and I would not like to have missed another opportunity of seeing the beautiful Acropolis. 'Seeing', though, implies that a visitor only experiences it with the eyes.

When we visit somewhere we say that we saw this or saw that place, which suggests that sight is the all-important sense. Yet what else can we say? How can we describe the experience of visiting a unique place like the hill on which the Acropolis stands? I 'experienced' it – too fanciful. Yet we hear and see and touch and smell, perhaps even taste the flavours of plants and herbs in the air – and we have other responses that are not of any senses. I imagine the past, for instance, and that also is part of my experience of a place. I certainly imagine the ghosts of citizens past. We also, I think, soak up something of the place in our very heart, in our souls.

3 April

The steamers and ferry boats in Greece depart so early in the morning one wonders why they don't simply leave the evening before! Our steamer for Itea was a ramshackle vessel which might once have been new – perhaps at the time of Nelson. Besides being ramshackle, it was also unbelievably crowded. Honestly, a troop ship is a haven of peace by comparison. Greek babies make even more noise than their parents, and this is saying a great deal. Floor space was scarce, and the hordes rushed up the gangplank as soon as the boat was ready, throwing down blankets and baggage to stake a space for themselves.

It is odd to me that in a country with such a beautiful climate, many people seem to spend most of their time indoors, in the shade. Most were quite happy to congregate in the gloom of the lower decks and passageways, blocking the aisles so that anyone who wanted to move had to step over breakfasts, children or boxes held together with string. Those forced by circumstance to make their journey on the upper deck in the sun seemed extremely annoyed at the prospect.

The air was crisp as we left the port of Piraeus, but by the time we had reached the Gulf of Corinth the sun was up and burning down quite strongly, causing most on the upper decks to cover themselves with headscarves, blankets, newspapers – indeed anything, whether suitable or not.

At Itea we disembarked, with myself as a sort of unofficial camp helper to the archaeological group, who had brought with them a great deal of equipment in addition to everyone's personal effects needed for a three-week stay.

Arrangements had been made in advance for the group to be met by, seemingly, about a hundred donkeys, and these beasts were milling round at Itea, causing great confusion and not a little mess at the harbour front. It also meant a shortage of donkeys for the Greeks who were getting off the steamer, so a great deal of arguing and haggling went on, the donkeys' owners reluctant to give up for less than a high price the trip to Delphi, which would be lucrative for them, especially by way of gratuities.

From Itea the battered road zig-zagged its way across the lower plain and then up towards Delphi, the hills and the slopes of Mount Parnassus. We passed through one village, causing great excitement, as if we were explorers in Africa, though groups of archaeological students must now have been making this trip for quite a number of years. But almost everything is made into some kind of occasion in Greece, it seems.

We are staying in a bustling village named Castri, close to the site of the temple. I had assumed 'Delphi' to be also the name of a town or village, but it refers just to the hillside site of the ancient temple and oracle. Castri used to be there too, in the same place as the antiquities, but it was moved. It is a large enough village, and busy, but still something of a contrast to life in Athens! The students eventually dispersed, and I went to find my own accommodation, having arranged to meet Anna in the early evening at a taverna close to the small square.

Finding a room was not in the least difficult, as the arrival of the string of donkeys brought out several young boys and old women, all anxious to see if rooms were needed. I would have thought that the students would have required all of the available places, but is seems it is early in the year yet for the summer visitors and other rooms are still empty. I looked at two rooms before discovering the one I have taken, which is perfect.

It is the upper part of a small house, but with its own outside stairway as entrance, rendering it completely private. The lavatory, which I must share with the family, does not bear description, but the room itself is clean and light.

Last night it proved its worth. We dined, the whole great group of us, in the taverna, and what an evening it proved to be. The crowd was additionally swollen by the curious come to see who we all were. Eventually, however, the rowdy party began to break up and, as we left at the very end, I had a chance to stroll peacefully arm-in-arm with Anna through the quiet white moonlit streets. We could have gone to her room, she said, though I have not yet seen this. Instead we chose mine, and climbed the uneven stairs rather carefully as we had both been enjoying the wine.

As I followed Anna up the stairs, I was watching her move, imagining her naked, and my shaft was already hardening from that picture in my mind and from the delicious memory of the previous week's pleasure. Then, I had not really known what was to happen, or imagined accurately the utter delight of it all, but last night as I climbed those stairs I knew, and the anticipation excited me.

As we entered the room and the door closed behind us, I grasped Anna in the darkness and kissed the back of her neck, feeling the soft downy blonde hair at the nape and imagining the soft taste of the hair elsewhere on her body. I pulled her hips to me, felt myself hard against her bottom, and bit her gently on the shoulder inside the collar of her dress. I cupped my hands over her breasts, then slid them down to her hips, and around to the front to hold that intimate part of her. She had her eyes closed, her head tilted to the ceiling, and her murmurs told me the pleasure she was feeling from my touches.

Bending slightly, I tugged her dress up so it bunched

around her waist, and my hands were able to caress the cool smooth skin of her inner thighs. She wore loose fitting pants, and my fingers went inside the legs of them, either side, and my fingertips met in the middle of her small tangle of hair, then slid down to the slit where the hair dampened and the skin became hot and swollen to the touch. I reached forward, my head over her shoulder, kissing her neck and cheek, and pushed my fingers deep between her legs as she parted them slightly to accommodate me. One finger slipped in, and Anna took a sharp intake of breath. She pushed her bottom against me now, back and forth, back and forth, rubbing me till I felt I would burst my trousers. I rubbed her in the rhythm of her movements, and we stayed that way for a moment, gently coaxing and pleasing each other.

The ache to be inside her body soon became so powerful to me, though, that I pulled down her pants beneath her dress, unbuttoned my trousers, and leant Anna forward against the bed while I took her from behind. The thrust of me inside her was intense, as she felt so tight around me, squeezing me firmly in the wet warmth of her. I revelled in the cool feel of her behind slapping against my stomach, and everything felt so good in this manner that it seemed a matter of seconds before I spurted inside her, again and again.

I knew Anna had not experienced the same pleasure this time with me as the previous time, and as soon as my mind cleared of the blinding haze that filled it, I wanted to love her again. She needed something too, and asked me to touch her. She lay on the bed, still mostly dressed, and pressed my fingers against her, where they sought for that bud of pleasure just inside of her. I found the swollen pearl and my fingers slid over it. And it was then that I recalled with a shock that I should have worn a sheath. In our desire I had forgotten, I continued to touch Anna, to gently slip and slide my fingers from side to side, knowing now where her most intense spot of pleasure lay, and stroking that taut flesh all around it before returning to the place, when she would whimper at the tender touch of it. As the whimpers became moans, and became more regular, I realised that she was starting to approach the peak of her pleasure and I stroked harder, concentrated on the one place, pressed her and rubbed her there, back and forth, back and forth, as fast as my fingers could manage, until at last her entire body tensed like the spring of a gun at the point of release, and she uttered a scream of joy. Every part of her seemed to twitch and tremble for a minute or more. All this in the complete blackness of the room, with no more than a shadowy sight of face or body.

'Hold me,' she said, and I held her tightly for a time, then we slipped off our clothes and climbed beneath the sheets to sleep in each other's arms. It was then I confessed I was sorry that I had forgotten to wear something, but she mumbled, half-asleep, that it didn't matter. This morning as we woke I mentioned it again, and she said that I was not to worry as it would be a safe time of the month for her (I do not know what those times are, and was a little too shy to admit to my ignorance) and besides, she added, sometimes it was worth the risk involved.

Life is for passion, she said, not for caution. She told me also that I was a good lover, that the English girls had obviously taught me well. I have not told her that I have made love with no-one else but her. Perhaps one day I will.

Now I shall walk up to Delphi itself. Anna had to attend an introductory talk this morning, followed by a welcoming lunch, but said she should be on the site this afternoon. Already I find it difficult to keep my hands from touching her, for at last I have discovered the joys of passion and can imagine no finer feeling in the world: I am consumed by it.

4 April

Yesterday, the ruins at Delphi itself. I made the walk from Castri – not too far for my damaged right leg, and pleasantly cool with the sky slightly clouded. Round a turn in the old road I was suddenly confronted by the ruins of the ancient sanctuary, but it was not the ruins which impressed me most, rather the view across the valley below. As I sat resting by the roadside and tried to take in the scale of the magnificence, a shaft of sunlight came between two clouds and ran the length of the valley, as one sometimes sees it racing across fields at home on a summer's day.

It is hard to describe the valley without being accused of exaggeration, but I think it is the most beautiful natural sight I have ever seen. The hills on either side are greening at this time of year, and they layer and overlap, while down on the valley floor are thousands of trees stretching away. You are drawn into the scene as if you were flying over an ancient forest, and I felt that I would like to swoop down that valley like a hawk and off over the sea to some mysterious place.

It is easy to see why the Apollo's oracle was consulted here. There can be no finer place for knowing the answers to necessary questions. I have so many questions myself, I almost wish the oracle were still alive.

I met with Anna at the site, and she was able to break off from her work for a time to walk with me and explain a little of the place and the ruins that are there. (All useful information to send to father!) I was impressed most by the theatre, where we sat on the hard stone benches as if witnessing one of the high classical tragedies on the almost circular stage below. Anna looked at me and we exchanged the gentlest of kisses, which was as arousing and enticing as her most passionate embrace. Anna said that if I liked this theatre, I should certainly visit the one at Epidavros, which is even more complete and impressive. Although I have only been here a few weeks, I can imagine spending a lifetime wandering in Greece. The classical world has always held a certain fascination for me, and the reality of being here is no disappointment. The theatre, like the Acropolis, has the power to summon up memories of the past, to make the ancients live again, and give us a sense of immortality.

The physical past is also still to be drawn out of Delphi, and Anna was able to tell me what is known already. I admit to being no great classical scholar, and without Anna would have stumbled around with my guide book, picking up small amounts of information here and there, merely recognising this or that building; but with someone knowledgeable to show the way one can learn so much more.

6 April

The days and nights pass slowly now, as if time is standing still, and I have a feeling that this idyllic life will last for ever. I spend the days walking, reading or thinking, or sometimes just sitting and looking. The weather is cooling a little, but still pleasant. Mikhalis told me that recently it has been exceptionally warm for so early in the year – although if it has been merely warm so far, I wonder how I shall react when July and August arrive.

Mikhalis runs a small café in Castri, which I have taken to frequenting. He is young, certainly younger than myself, and the café did belong to his father until he was recently killed in some kind of explosion – Mikhalis couldn't or perhaps wouldn't explain this properly. He has only recently started learning English, which he will need for foreigners in the café, so we attempt to teach each other a little when the place is not busy. This belongs now to his mother, who does the cooking in the tiniest of kitchens; but Mikhalis, who serves and organises, wants somehow to get out of the village and go to Athens or even England or America. He wants to see the larger world but, of course, I am sworn to secrecy on this dream, for he does not know how his mother would react to his going, which perhaps would mean selling the café.

Mikhalis does not know what he really wants to do, except work and earn money, and see what freedom life has to offer outside the village here. Yet, to go, he will need money of the sort he will never earn here. He swears he will go to Athens first, earn some money there, enough to take him wherever he wishes then to go, or perhaps even buy himself a business in Athens.

I hope that he achieves his ambitions – when he discovers what his ambitions are – but what, I wonder, will happen to him in the years to come? Will he escape Castri? Will he perhaps only get as far away as washing dishes in an Athens restaurant and never move from there? Or even meet a foreign woman here and fall in love and marry, to be taken down another unexpected path to places of which he has not yet heard?

8 April

I am writing this at the small table in my upstairs room, in the early evening, listening to the rain beating down on the dark earth outside. Anna left a few moments ago to attend a lecture meeting. The school could not work outdoors today because of this constant rain, and most students were left to their own devices to study or write up reports. I have no idea what Anna can report of this afternoon, as we spent the time naked in the bed behind me, discovering new ways of pleasing each other.

This morning I ran through the muddy streets to eat breakfast at Mikhalis's, then dashed back through the rain to my room, holding my waterproof over my head. I read some Housman, then re-read my diary to date, becoming quite excited again at the descriptions of my times with

Anna. They repeat constantly in my mind, what justification can there be for recording them? Yet they also anticipate for me the time to come, like this afternoon.

It surprised me to hear a knock on the door, and to see a rather wet and bedraggled Anna almost fall into the room in her haste to escape the downpour. She told me immediately that they would not be working today and that she had spent the morning writing up a report, and so her day now was free until six o'clock. She removed her coat and kicked off her shoes, putting them by the door to dry beside my own.

Then Anna lay on my bed and sighed, 'Oh thank God,' and told me that she sorely needed me to hold her. I was happy to oblige, and quick to suggest that feeling skin against skin would be even better. Anna smiled quietly, and we undressed and held each other in the bed, not in a passionate manner but softly, stroking and comforting each other and enjoying the feel of being honest and naked and natural together.

We talked for a time, lying face to face, and our words circled around the subject of the future, until I cupped her bottom in my hand, and as I stroked I could not stop my fingers straying very gently, almost not touching, the soft hair between her legs and the sweet folds of skin beneath.

'Nice,' I remember her murmuring. It was marvellous to know we had the whole afternoon ahead of us, and no need to hurry.

At some point as we lay touching and caressing, Anna asked, 'Will you kiss me?' I moved across to kiss her lips, but she stopped me and said 'No, there, where your fingers are touching.'

I kissed her on the neck, between her breasts, on the tip of each swollen nipple, then brushed my lips across her flat stomach and then down to the edge of the honey hair. I admit that I was not sure what to do, but I was intrigued by the chance to kiss her in this secret private place. As I moved down the bed to lay between her legs, the sheets were pushed back and fell to the floor, leaving us both exposed. I kissed her first on the inside of each thigh, then held her hips with my hands as I moved to kiss the edge of those open lips before me.

That part of her fascinated me. I had often touched her quim and felt it swell, had been inside Anna there, yet had never looked closely. It had its own peculiar beauty. Two glistening lips, framed by wisps of golden hair. I first touched one with my tongue, then the other and could suddenly feel the shudders that went through Anna as I did so. I licked again, and kissed, then nibbled with my teeth, tugging the skin a little. I spread the swelling lips apart with my fingers, to discover inner lips, looking more delicate and vulnerable, and at the top folds of skin hiding that tiny hard bud which gives Anna such pleasure.

I licked her there, pressed the tip of my tongue hard against it, passed my probing tongue back and forth in the way I often passed my fingers over it, and this seemed to give Anna even more pleasure.

I kissed her outer lips, then the inner lips, then her private mound, moving my tongue faster and harder the more Anna began to writhe.

Anna began to move so much, so violently, that it was hard for my lips to maintain their contact between her legs – at times she would wrestle and jerk as if trying to throw me off, but she would grab my head and press me back to her, sometimes pressing my mouth so hard against her wetness that I was sure I must hurt. Yet still she pressed me to her, and if I pressed my teeth against her mound it seemed to arouse her the more, causing her to thrash and moan; so I forced my mouth ever harder against her, swallowing her gaping lips, taking them in my own, nibbling at them, then licking at her very quickly for a time, being gentle then hard. And then just when I felt every muscle in my mouth was sore from the work, I sensed that she was nearing her moment of intensest pleasure, and so I thrust in my tongue again and again, swamped her mound with my mouth, and rubbed my mouth round and round against her till she pushed her hips hard upwards in a spasm of delight and gave out the deepest and longest of groans I had heard from her, one that eventually died in her throat as her whole body sank back into the crumpled sheets and lay there trembling.

I kissed her once again briefly, but she shuddered away, telling me not to, as she was too tender. My mouth was wet with her fluid, my chin and cheeks soaked in the juice of her as I lay my head against the pillow of her thighs and closed my eyes and rested.

My own arousal had come and then disappeared again as I concentrated on pleasing her, but after a few minutes while we both lay and listened to the rain, she stroked me and coaxed me till my shaft stiffened in her hand. This time we remembered to take care. When I had entered her, she lifted her legs and encircled my hips with them, also squeezing me deep inside her which gave me such pleasure that I spurted almost at once, joyous to be filling her and feeling one with her.

And so our wet afternoon passed, and I pleased her again with my fingers this time. My own arousal would not reappear, although now I can feel it once more.

I must put my pen aside now and brave the rain. For I am to meet my Anna and dine with her and return here to spend my night beside her.

11 April

When everything is so good, how, I ask, can it quickly go so wrong? It is now lunchtime and I write alone in my upstairs room. I cannot understand it, no matter how much I try. And the harder I try, the less I understand.

The last few days have passed splendidly. The storm blew itself out, the sun resumed shining, and Anna and I continued to explore each other's delights at night, while during the day she worked on the site and I explored the half wild countryside around, with long walks through the slopes, savouring the warm ever-changing scent of blossoming herbs and flowers. I did not even feel the inclination to record these things, indulging in a spell of appreciation of life, rather than constantly needing to write it down lest it fade away.

This morning we awoke beside each other as has become usual, or seemingly so; yet there was a guarded silence about Anna, a certain lack of response when I spoke to her: a sombre 'Yes' or 'No' where normally there would be a smile and brief conversation. I asked her immediately what was wrong, but Anna insisted, 'Nothing.' When I persisted – gently, I thought – that something must be the matter, she quickly became angry, asking me how would I know what she was thinking, and was I capable of seeing into her mind? I only wish that I was.

A few moments later, after assuring me that nothing was wrong, she began to talk, though still in a flat, aggressive manner. It seems that last night in the taverna I mentioned to a friend of hers that I was looking forward to experiencing the rest of Greece – especially Epidavros, which Anna had recently recommended to me. Although Anna told me that I *must* see it, it seems that she does not really want me to do that. She understood my comment to mean that I would soon be moving on. In reply, I told Anna that when she insisted I must see Epidavros I assumed she was telling me – obliquely, to be true – that she was not expecting us to spend the summer together.

True, I have not yet given enough thought to what the immediate future holds, but I explained to Anna that I was happy to live in the present, and when the time came for her party to return to Athens, we should decide then. For myself, I did not want to part from her, and wanted to go back with her to Athens so that we could be together.

Then Anna said I must not do that, that my life should not revolve around hers, and that I must make my own decisions and do what I came to do, which is to see the rest of Greece. By this time I was unnerved and beginning to see red, for not ten minutes earlier she had been upset because she thought my life was *not* merely going to revolve around hers, because I had said I was looking forward to seeing Epidavros.

'What I want is to be with you,' I told Anna, but she tearfully insisted that she knew it wasn't. So, in turn, I asked her if she was capable of seeing into my mind. This upset her, and in a silence as oppressive as the brooding calm before our recent thunderstorm, she dressed and left my room.

The words of our argument are going round and round in my mind. She contradicts herself. She wants me, she doesn't want me. I must stay, I must go. I must visit Epidavros, I must not visit Epidavros. This so complicates everything. The honest thing is to do what I want to do – if only I knew what that was.

Today is Sunday. Though I have not been inside a church since I left the army and I know little of the Orthodox rites, perhaps a little calm will help straighten out my thoughts, which at the moment are as untidy as a tangled ball of string with no end and no beginning.

Eating alone this evening was the strangest part of today. I chose to eat at Mikhalis's, as at least there would be someone to talk to and neither myself, Anna nor the others normally eat there in the evenings. Of course Mikhalis was busy for much of the time, not so much with people eating there as with the local men drinking and playing cards, which seems to involve a great deal of table-slapping every time a card is played. The Greeks do not seem to eat away from their houses much: although to us the taverna is remarkably cheap, for them, with not a great deal of money, it is even cheaper to stay at home. Yet the men still find money for their drinking! I suppose that is the same everywhere, and here in the Mediterranean the men must have their dignity in front of the others. A hen-pecked Greek husband would live a miserable existence.

Late in the evening, one of the shepherds, a large man with a great deal of wine and rough brandy inside him, stood at the bar and began to chant a vigorous song, accompanied by hand-clapping from the others, very regular and loud. Everyone joined in, some singing while playing cards, rejoicing in the chance to bang down the playing of a card in time with one of the hand-claps of the song. The singer, very unshaven, his black trousers tied with coarse string and forever on the verge of descent, brought out a rather tattered handkerchief, which he held dramatically above his head as he started to dance – very elegantly, transforming him for a moment into a symbol of joy and grace. (Though who am I to say that he is not one always, judging him simply by his clothes? That same joy and grace must still be inside when the man is not drunk and dancing.) The dancer was joined by others in the centre of the taverna, one grasping the handkerchief, others grasping hands in a row that became sometimes a line, sometimes a circle, the singing and rhythmic clapping continuing all the while. The dance involved a frequent drop to the knee, like a curtsy, and then the circle would break and the men duck and weave under bridges formed by the linked arms, as they were raised in the air. Just when the movements were getting faster all the while, hypnotic, quicker and quicker as if the dance could go nowhere and do nothing but disappear into a whirlwind of noise and dust, one of the men fell and the dance broke up in ribald laughter and jeering.

My head was full of dance, noise and not a little retsina as I walked back towards my room. Then I saw Anna and several of her friends in the main street, evidently making their own way home. She saw me and turned her back, laughing rather too loudly at some chance remark, obviously intent on showing me what a time she could have without me. So let her enjoy herself if she wishes.

13 April

Yesterday I walked away from Castri, knowing I could now go wherever I wished, and decided to let chance be my guide. It has not taken me that far! I walked for a time along a track ascending the slopes, until a man riding one thin mule and leading another overtook me and offered a hefty slice of bread – though slice is altogether too smooth a word for the jagged hunk that he ripped from his coarse loaf. He repeated something, which I now know to be the name of this village, Arakova, and when I shrugged to say that I did not care, he indicated to me to climb onto the rear mule and so it was that after a bumpy journey I arrived here.

We dismounted in the centre of the village, and he shook my hand before leading his mules away down one of the narrow side-alleys. Scarcely a word had we spoken, yet great goodwill had passed between us.

We are distinctly higher, the air has cooled noticeably and as we were riding on the mules, I noticed several mountain birds of prey wheeling high overhead.

I dropped my bags at the entrance to the nearest café, and was at once greeted by a word I have come to know well.

Thomatio, which means a room.

Ne, I said, showing a masterful command of the language, and I was led, not into but out of the small café and along the street to a rather drab private house where the café owner left me to the attention of, I guessed, his wife. I was led, as I have now become accustomed, out of the house and up a narrow stone staircase to a dingy room above. This was considerably less impressive than the ones I had seen so far, and I realised I had previously been somewhat lucky and rather spoiled. This room has straw and dirt on the bare stone floor, and a piece of rush matting rolled in a corner – evidently the sleeping arrangements. The woman said something which I imagine was to do with blankets, for indeed she placed one in the room later that day – for I did agree to take it, as I have slept in worse places than this, and there is not a great amount of choice in a village of this size.

Last night was rather cold – the window has no covering, the lopsided wooden door has more holes than the window, and the roof more holes than the door. Scarcely a little 'love nest', but there is no possibility of using it for that purpose. I begin to miss Anna a little, but then I remember the argument, the rest of this summer that I have before me and most of all the harsh way she ignored me in the street.

If you can behave like that towards someone, how can you possibly care for them? Memories like that tell me I am right to have left. There must be plenty of other women, travellers or students like Anna all over Greece. Although certainly not here in Arakova, judging by my observations so far.

Not that I want to indulge in a dalliance with some black-weeded widow. Nor do I imagine, for a moment, that if any of them were young and attractive, custom would allow them to become in any way involved with a foreigner. I do not think Arakova will detain me for very long!

I have discovered that from here (as from Delphi) it is possible in mid-summer to make the ascent to the peaks of Mount Parnassus, which is about 8,000 feet in height, the main peak being known in Greek as *Wolf Mountain*, a beautifully evocative name. The snow is often too heavy to enable an ascent to be made readily at any time other than the months of July or August. I have met here a guide, again called Ianni, a tough-looking goatherd, who says he will take me tomorrow if I wish, but the ones who were roughly translating for me advised against this, saying he is a madman. I have not come to Greece to be abandoned in snow and eaten by wolves; nor to go higher where the air is colder. I can be cold well enough in England. My fancy is to study my tattered maps and books, take advice and find somewhere warm – or at the very least head a little further south.

17 April

According to the map I am at least a few degrees further south, and nearer sea level, and my heart feels warmer than it did in Arakhova. I am now in Missolonghi, where Lord Byron died nearly a hundred years ago, he who was 'mad, bad and dangerous to know'. It is a surprisingly large town, and indeed I am rather surprised to be here. 'Let chance be your guide' – this will govern my travelling from now on. I walked back to Itea on Wednesday (I believe days are starting to lose their meaning), to see if I could book a steamer back to Athens, with the intention of then going on to visit some of the many Aegean islands, but no steamer was due within the next three days so I sat at a café to have a glass of beer before looking to find a room to hire while I waited. An elderly gentleman at the next table, who had heard me speaking English, paid for the beer when it arrived – a typical gesture that still pleases but now no longer surprises me.

The man was perhaps in his late sixties, though it is hard to be accurate about age here in the South where sun leathers the skin and harsh work can make a man of thirty appear fifty. This man was comparatively well-dressed, his dark suit almost new, and he had that air of being well-to-do. He was quietly spoken and addressed me in English, saying he had heard me ask about the ferry to Athens. He told me that whatever I wished to know about boats in Greece I should ask him. For he had sailed not only to every main port in Greece but everywhere in the world, had realised his ambition of being a Captain of his own steamer, and had come back to his home port of Itea to live out the rest of his life in comfort.

The Captain was proud of his command of English (and five other languages, he told me), and I think very much enjoyed showing it off in his mild-mannered way. He was well respected in the port, many a passer-by raised a hand to greet him from the street. So I bought him a beer in turn as we continued to talk. He had never married, he said, which was his one regret now that he was old and alone, but his wife had always been the sea. Don't be old and alone, he advised me with a sad smile.

When he discovered that I had the whole summer ahead of me, and that I was to become again an undergraduate in the autumn, he told me to forget about Athens, dismissing it with a contemptuous and bitter twist of the mouth.

'Go the other way,' was his advice, 'go straight to Missolonghi.'

'Why so?' I said in surprise.

'Do you not admire your Lord Byron?' he asked me. I assured him that I did, and had planned to visit the town at some point if it proved possible. 'Possible?' he said. 'Anything is possible, you simply do it.' He pointed to a boat lying at anchor about fifty yards from the sea wall, and to a tubby man in a thick blue sweater. That man, the Captain assured me, would take me to Turlis, very close to Missolonghi.

Which indeed he did, though it was quite a journey, heading out into the dark Mediterranean, partly at night, in the man's fishing boat – a large boat, but one on which sleeping still proved rather difficult. I did not object to being under the stars, they were beautiful, nor the hardness of the planks, far rather that than the soft mud of the trenches, it was the chug of the engine combined with the smell of oil and stale fish that proved not to provide the ideal setting. Yet I would not have missed a trip in that manner. It makes me feel I am here, part of the country, if only for a short time.

19 April

Missolonghi is not a typical Greek town, at least not as I have been told they are or imagine them to be, but I like it. It is fringed by shallow lagoons, which in the early morning can smell rather foul, although either the scent disperses during the day or my nose simply gets used to the odour. It is also a rather ramshackle town, not the heroic site one associates with the War of Inependence and the death of George Byron.

I recall a rare evening spent at an inn table behind the lines with Sassoon and Goodall in (Amiens? Abbeville?), talking poets and poetry, art and writing, the idiocy of staff officers, soldiers and poets. Anything but the inescapable fighting. Inevitably enough the name of Byron dropped into the conversation. Opinions as to his merits differed, but all agreed on the wild and glorious nature of his life, and all admired the way in which he lived it to the full in accordance with his own beliefs, no matter if these might seem misguided or not.

Missolonghi had become a mythical place to us, even the very sound of the word seemed to evoke bravado and courage, yet the place is completely ordinary – and is this not more fitting?

'Courage' is seen as a noble aim, but does it not come out of the ordinary, everyday, mundane life that surrounds us? Bravery takes place in ramshackle surroundings in ditches rife with rats, in dusty barns and damp farmyards, and 'noble' deaths take place in drab towns that lie by unpleasant lagoons.

If ever the others come to visit Missolonghi and sit here and look at it and reflect, I hope they recall that brave, brief evening we shared.

22 April

The more events that happen, the less time there is in which to write: or less inclination? But that is always the way of my diaries. I remember every year as a boy faithfully starting my Christmas-present diary on 1 January with a full and glowing account of that day's activities, of resolutions to be kept. Gradually through the weeks to come what was written would diminish, till by this time of year it would contain nothing more elaborate than 'Mother's birthday' or 'visited the Trenchards'.

Mention of mother reminds me that I had better write to her, having told them both that I would be staying in Delphi till further notice. Doubtless there is a letter lying there for me – what will happen to it? Thrown out, I suppose, if uncollected. I must arrange to get some additional money, too. At least there is a bank here, so I hope that arranging a transfer of remittance from Athens will not take too long.

I must admit that I did not come to Greece expecting to find a series of romances. I half-imagined that perhaps I might meet some delicate young English woman travelling with her parents, that an innocent flirtation would follow, perhaps even to be taken up again in England when it might proceed beyond the hand holding, kiss on cheek stage. I did not dare imagine anything so startling as the encounter with Anna, which has both opened my eyes and fired my body. I realise now what my life might have missed, had things happened only slightly differently in France.

Even before I saw the book that she was reading, I sensed that the neatly-dressed woman sitting alone in the café was English. It was good to have this confirmed as I passed her table and saw that the volume was of Byron's verse – of course, what else could it have been in this town? Before my affair with Anna, I would not have had the courage to stop and speak, I would have passed quietly by in my polite English manner and left the woman undisturbed. Anna has given me great confidence in myself, however, and has also awakened desires within me. I will admit that I stopped to speak out of a kind of physical as well as mental curiosity.

'An *aficionado* of Byron?' I asked, a simple enough means of making friendly contact with someone, something which so often escapes us. Her look in reply was one for which the word 'demure' must have been invented, so exact is that adjective, but she did at least smile and say 'Yes,' before adding that she was surprised to meet another English person here. We exchanged a few polite words of explanation, and then I asked if she would mind my sitting at her table, to talk with her and have a drink.

'Please,' she said.

I insisted at once that I did not wish to intrude – of course, I did – and then told her in detail of my first thoughts on Missolonghi, leading on to my brief meeting with Sassoon and Goodall, and my reflections on Byron and the myth surrounding a death in what turned out to be such a very ordinary place. Partly this was said because I felt I needed to keep talking, but partly also because it was marvellous to share these thoughts and have someone respond – particularly a woman who was curious indeed that I had met Sassoon, though I think a little disappointed that it was only a passing acquaintance between an officer and a trooper and one that had not been kept up.

She had read and admired the *War Poems*, those published last year, and was keen to hear every word I could recall of his opinion on Byron, a particular literary hero of hers. She is on what can only be described as a pilgrimage, to see the places in Greece that are associated with that poet, and Missolonghi is her last stopping place – for one week – before she returns to England to resume her job as a private governess – an envious job, it seems with a noble but cultured family who sound rather pleasant and allow her to make frequent breaks of a literary nature.

It is a great pleasure to talk to someone in English again after several days – my words and thoughts get caught inside my head and swirl in the mind when I have no outlet for them. Writing them down helps, but there is no match for an intelligent and responsive listener.

23 April

Mary is a Byron expert of some depth and we walked together yesterday to visit several sites associated with him, and lingered in the gardens near the town's main gate where an imposing statue to the poet marks the famous spot where his very heart is buried. Though we had both already visited there, we went again to see the house where he died, and to sit nearby on a stone bench and look at ancient trees that he too might have gazed upon. To be English in Missolonghi is to be welcomed everywhere.

To my delight, it seems that Mary's admiration for the soldier poet enhances my attraction in her eyes, though the 'poet' aspect of the description is not something I would apply to myself. I try to write, but I know that I seldom achieve the inexplicable mystery that lies at the heart of a good poem. As I have noted before, some of my work pleases me, but mainly because it captures the memory of an event or a feeling. The verse equivalent of a simple photograph. Sassoon is a poet, his friend Graves is a poet, and both were kind and encouraging when they saw the half-hearted efforts of myself and others, but to be a poet is something which you *know*. That is your destiny, and it is not mine, whatever else mine might be.

At the moment I shall content myself with describing Mary – how different from Anna, not merely in appearance but in temperament, too. Mary is taller, also slim but her features more angular with long black hair that frames the pale skin of her face. Where Anna was boisterous, with laughter never far from the surface, Mary is more serious and talks more quietly – more typically English, I suppose. Not that she is without humour, but one has to strain sometimes to catch the quietly teasing comment made with straight face, the understated remark. Nor does Mary shy away from physical contact, but where Anna was more direct, I think Mary plays the courting game; very English, to obey the rules and proceed at the right pace even in another country. Just as I would have myself with Anna, had Anna not shown me another way.

Last night we dined together in a quiet restaurant and spoke again of the artists and writers we admired. Mary quizzed me gently about my slight limp and asked about the war and my own experiences. I feel I could perhaps talk to her further, as there is much to talk about, but intimacy is needed to open one's heart to the gaze of others, and as yet we have but a few days' friendship. Mary suggested I should write and try to have published an account of my time in the army: to keep it simple, the words of an 'ordinary' soldier who lived through that most awful and momentous time on the Somme. Would that I had kept these diaries then, as some did who dared to break the rules, scribbling away in secret with stubs of pencil on scraps of paper in the frequent spells of inactivity.

Yet now, thank God, I am more concerned with the

present and the future than the past. I can imagine nothing more important and pleasing just now than to persuade Mary to share a bed and to indulge again in those new pleasures. I find myself growing hard as I try to picture her lean body, which is always well-hidden beneath high-necked blouses and long dresses. But if I wish to see rather than imagine, then I must act rather than think.

Last night as I escorted her back to her simple hotel after our meal, I put my arm around her small waist, and she made no objection. At the darkened door to the hotel she turned to thank me for walking back with her, and for the evening and the meal. I made sure to keep my hand on her waist, and with the other gently eased her face towards me as I leant to her lips and kissed her briefly and softly. The moment was charged – that point when friendship becomes intimacy, an act acknowledged with fear and excitement, leading to the unknown. And tonight we dine together again.

25 April

Sunday, and Mary wishes to bathe herself and wash some of her clothing, so I have returned for a few hours to the small room I have taken in a rundown seafront hotel.

It was when? Friday evening after we dined? I made an offer to escort her home, although I made the deliberate and not very subtle mistake of saying that I would see her to her room, then quickly corrected myself and said 'hotel' instead. I got a very brief smile that seemed to me to say 'Really?'

in undecided curiosity.

As we walked back through the darkened streets I said that it was a great pity that such a beautiful evening had to end, and as Mary agreed, I suggested we make the walk last by going via the gate and the public gardens where Byron's statue stands. On our way we passed the café where we had met, and the very same table was empty, so on impulse we sat down and ordered a brandy – French cognac – to celebrate our good fortune in meeting.

Mary said politely but with feeling that I had made her stay in Missolonghi a happier one – she was content to travel alone if need be, but a sympathetic companion enriched the experience immeasurably. I said less originally that I would drink to that thought.

Abandoning our visit to the statue and garden, we walked arm-in-arm towards her hotel, and I guided us through a narrow grove of trees beside the road where we were sheltered from view. There we paused and I turned abruptly to hold her in my arms. We kissed, softly at first but then more passionately, and when I edged my tongue between her softening lips I was pleased to see that she responded, as she did when I pressed my hands against the small of her back to bring her hips against mine. She pushed against me, the soft area between her hips rubbing back and forth a little, as a cat might get its pleasure by rubbing against one's legs. Through the thickness of her clothing I was sure I could feel her soft mound pressed firmly against me.

Even in a secluded spot late at night it is impossible to be passionate but chaste for too lengthy a time. We ceased kissing but still held each other, and she looked down for a while before raising her eyes to gaze at me – not out of any sense of shame, I was sure, but from not knowing what was to happen next. We were travelling in uncharted waters. I felt it was for me to do the leading.

'I would like to kiss you again,' I told her, 'over every inch of your body.' At which she closed her eyes, and I could see her imagining the act in the slightness of her smile.

'Would you?' she quietly asked. My answer was that yes, I would, but my drab room was neither clean nor inviting.

'I have a comfortable room, quite an expensive hotel room,' she said, with a wry smile.

'With a night porter guarding the door against unwanted visitors?' I reminded her. But she said: 'And a french window that opens onto a low balcony, which I am sure a young man like you would have no trouble in climbing.'

Indeed the climb was little trouble, but though the balcony overlooked a small, unlit side-street, I was still nervous about what a passer-by or policeman would have made of the unusual scene if they had turned into that street in the few seconds or so that it took to pull myself up and over the iron surround, which was thankfully sturdily built. Perhaps it was intended for this purpose!

Her room was astonishingly comfortable – containing not only the usual scant bed and washstand but a comfortable armchair, small writing bureau, dark wardrobe, unfrayed carpet, and an oil painting on the wall. I turn to Mary as she closed the shutters behind me, clasped my arms around her waist, and again insisted that I would like to kiss every inch of her body. I began with her lips, and slowly kissed her cheeks, her chin, her forehead and around her neck. The smooth delicate skin at the side of her neck was sensitive and I could feel her shivering at the touch.

I opened gently the first few buttons of her white blouse, and kissed the bones of her neck and then unbuttoned some more pearl buttons to reveal the pale slopes of her breasts, where I placed my lips and kissed and licked the soft whiteness. Her blouse fell to the floor, leaving her shoulders and arms bare, until they were covered in my kisses.

All this time she stood, completely passive, only moving her arms to let me remove her blouse, her dark eyes mostly closed as she responded with a delightful selfish pleasure to the attentions on her body. I unbuckled her skirt and that also fell to the floor, revealing her whole body before me, dressed in white cotton, till this too joined the crumpled clothing at her feet on the carpet, and she stood smiling as I kneeled before her and kissed her legs, and feet, fulfilling my promise of attending to every inch of her.

I bent to kiss her feet, her ankles and then moved my lips slowly up her beautiful legs, crawling behind and round her in a spiralling motion trying to reach every part. As I pressed my lips to her thighs, she parted her legs in silence and I was able to bury my mouth in the tangle of her black hair, until silver beads of juice nestled in the curls. When my tongue pushed between those other lips she held my head to her and a tremor of pleasure passed all the way up her body. She moved away and lay back on her bed, as I began swiftly to remove my clothing in order to join her, but she said that my mission of kissing was not complete as I had not touched the base of her back or her buttocks, and she turned over while I kissed her there, in the hollow of her back, then over the taut rising mounds of her bottom, at which she lifted towards me, presenting herself to me. I quickly put on my sheath and pushed myself into her wetness, as I had done with Anna, but moving more gently, slowly in and out, and it was excitement to my eyes as well as my body to watch with fascination the way my shaft would disappear deep inside her, emerging again as if caressed by her swollen lips.

I held her slim hips firmly and she moved her bottom rhythmically against me, sighing from time to time. I love that exquisite conjunction of bodies, the slap of the backs of her thighs against me, the slap as her bottom pushes against the hair of my groin, and I was torn between the intense desire to spurt deep into her, and the desire to make the pleasure last for longer and longer, and to wait till she too was ready to join me in that spasm of supreme pleasure. Each time the feeling of excitement approached, I slowed as if beginning anew and then built again, then slowed, till Mary's panting breath became quicker and quicker and she said 'Mmmm, yes . . .' as I thrust harder and faster knowing her climax was seconds away, and it came in a glorious moment when my head seemed to fill with swirling silver mists and my ears were drowned with Mary's sudden cries and my body full of the feel of her squeezing me uncontrollably.

We slept a satisfying sleep, and loved again in the early morning while lying side by side, our legs entangled tautly in a lover's knot. We could lie together no longer, I made my escape by dropping over the low balcony (with Mary on watch as I now lacked the protection of darkness), and we arranged to meet later, in that small place with its cluster of wooden chairs we now call 'our café'.

Yesterday was passed pleasantly in the warm sun. Our physical intimacy has created a new relaxed friendliness between us, and we talked lightly as we walked out of the town's outskirts to picnic among the olive groves – away from the ever-present sour smell from the surrounding lagoons. A famous shrine to Byron or not, I would not care to be here in the height of the summer. Mary talks matter-of-factly and a little enviously about my staying here and travelling the Aegean in total freedom, and talks equally easily about her own return and her work with her – quite famous – family in London. Mary insists that if she were me she would never return, and although this was said in the euphoria of the moment, I too have those feelings – if only!

It is strange to sit in the dust beneath an ancient olive tree and talk to a person who can appear at some moments to be an utter stranger to you, and yet know that the previous evening both of you were as naked and as close as two people have ever been. I like Mary's mild shyness and the hesitant way that she asks if I might send her the occasional postcard from here (as if a letter would perhaps be too presumptuous). I told her that I would – and I will. And perhaps see her too when I return – as we will not be too far apart.

Tired of writing this down, I would like to walk among the groves, then to sit, to read this again, to drink wine, to think, to bask in the warm glory of simply being here and being happy for the first time in so many years.

1 May

Reading over again my first night with Mary, and thinking of the times together which are not described, I feel aroused once more. I sent her a picture postcard today, as I promised, one I had bought in Missolonghi showing a view of the house where Byron died. On the reverse side, I made a rather oblique reference to the balcony of her hotel room, such that anyone else reading the card would regard it as totally innocent.

When I left Missolonghi, I made arrangements for any mail I was awaiting to be forwarded, having been recommended to take a steamer down the rugged western coast to Kalamata, which is a lively port with a holiday air tucked in to one of the deep bays of the wild southern coast, the Peloponnisos as it is called. (My Greek is coming along quite well now, and I can remember the words for a great number of the objects that I come across in the course of travelling, though conversational sentences still prove a little more difficult.)

By the time any mail from home catches up wherever I am, I think my parents will both have despaired of me – having said I would be in Delphi till further notice, then probably back in Athens, they will have received my missive from Missolonghi, complete with reference to Byron, and now a further one saying I am leaving for Kalamata. I can imagine them thinking that I am being chased around Greece by brigands – both were so convinced that this trip would be my downfall. If only they knew how happy I really am – I try hard to convey that in the letters and postcards, but somehow the more one insists that something is true, the more it seems that the opposite must be the case.

The ride in the ferry was another occasion of note. As the battered vessel arrived and tied up at Missolonghi, all the would-be passengers attempted to embark across a single gangplank while those on board were still leaving the boat. The vessel was bouncing a little on the swell, and I am amazed that no-one was pitched into the water, especially the stout ladies in their black dresses, with their several boxes and bags tied in ragged bundles with string, or the others who ushered hens, sheep and goats aboard, or struggling painfully with every item of house furniture imaginable. Why there should have been such a flurry to get on board when the boat was not due to leave for a further hour I cannot tell. It seems a total contrast to the normal Greek lack of concern with hurry or timetables. The ferry may come today or it may come tomorrow, and we will catch it when it comes, why worry, sit here and have a drink – such is the general attitude. Yet when a boat or bus does arrive, there is a frenzied fight to clamber aboard as if, as it were, devil take the hindmost – understandable if seats were limited, but the steamer would easily hold twice as many as eventually did travel upon it.

A black-dressed woman no bigger than a large pixie was transporting a wooden crate the size of a coffin, yelling at the porters, telling them to get it across the gangplank without damage and be quick about it – at least, that was what I understood her frenzy to be about.

We called in at several small ports along this stretch of beautiful mountained coast, where scenes of great excitement

A.N.A.D.—5

were enacted every time, as if we were the Second Coming itself. There are a surprising number of foreigners like myself, all travelling in varying degrees of comfort and with varying quantities of luggage. But though I was by now (I admit) keeping a keen eye open for any unattached female traveller, none seemed to join the boat. Yet I am certain in a town such as Kalamata, there will be foreign women. After all, this is one of the main ports of this part of Greece, with a wide harbour that bobs pleasantly with boats of all shapes and sizes, and there is that jaunty slightly wicked air of ports everywhere, and a rugged coast with plenty of opportunity for bathing.

I have not yet plunged into the dark sea, and when I have had the chance today to trail my fingers in the water it was rather cold, despite the heat of the day. The weather now is glorious, and my skin has browned quite noticeably. Before I left, everyone advised me to take care in hot climates, yet I imagine my skin was well hardened to the sun's effects in France, for not all the time was mud and rain, and there were several hot stretches. Unfortunately, these are associated in my mind with a furious increase in the number of burials.

3 May

In two days it will be my birthday, and although I had anticipated a quiet time it appears that this may be celebrated in some style after all, thanks to the inveterate hospitality of the Greeks. It is so easy to make friends here, particularly now that I can speak something of the language. My days with the grammar book have at last been repaid.

Returning to the subject of my birthday, I was very fortunate recently to meet a group of young Greeks in one of the bars, fishermen for the most part, yet more stylishly turned out than one might expect on what must be the meagre pickings of their occupation. They are boisterous and amusing, and give me a certain respect due to my lone travelling and my soldiering past. Many speak some English, and we communicate well enough, in a simple kind of way. Enough anyway to enjoy a joke and a drink, and to share an eye for the ladies. One is allowed to see little of the young single Greek women, as these tend to stay very much at home; helping their mothers with the housework or looking after young children – already learning their place in the Greek world. Slightly older married women, however, pass by in the street beside their husbands, and there are a number of foreign women too, the more attractive among these eliciting comments from the boys, not all of which they choose to translate for me, which is perhaps just as well. But when I told them it was to be my birthday on Wednesday, they vowed we would celebrate in a manner I would never forget. Whether this is wise remains to be seen!

7 May

Whether it was wise, I am still not sure! We had a rowdy

meal before the boys took me to an old Greek taverna in the deepest back streets for a brandy – I think my final total was only three, but it is hard to be sure as the glasses at our table were continually topped up whenever we rose to join in the wild dancing – yes, I was hauled up and taught a few rudimentary steps and danced in the taverna with the others, my arms around shoulders on either side, forming a solid line that bent and bobbed and rose again in one movement – almost in one movement. Let us say that it was flat as the sea is flat, but had a tendency to roll occasionally. To what would have been my embarrassment, had I been sober, I was called upon to give a solo dance in honour of my birthday, which I did, but thankfully it was enthusiasm rather than expertise that was sought and appreciated.

After a couple of hours the boys decided it was time to move on – the male company in the battered taverna was all very well for the old men, it seemed, but not for the younger ones, who had other interests. So we left the taverna and walked down towards the harbour and through the glass doors of what seemed a rather more sophisticated private club. Certainly there were a number of people there who appeared well-at-heel, and I realised at once that they went with the private boats and yachts which occupied part of the harbour. It was not long before I was incapable of seeing anything. Suffice it to say that I was introduced to the dubious pleasures of *raki*, which was described to me as being made from the dregs of ouzo, or something along those lines. It contains, I was proudly told, all those things that line the bottom of a barrel when the ouzo is drained away –

skin, pips, stalks, and, for all I know, dead mosquitoes and other wildlife. It certainly has a bite like a barrel full of mosquitoes.

Certain pictures I can recall – of tables being pushed together, of flamboyant offers to take me to Italy, Crete, Egypt, Athens, of more and wilder dancing, of quietly leaving the group for a time to be violently sick in a dark alleyway (for the first time in several years, but feeling much the better afterwards), and of later dancing, quite intimately, with a small charming Frenchwoman of about 35 on whose bed I awoke yesterday morning with not the slightest idea of how I came to be there. I know that nothing more intimate than dancing had taken place – or if it had then the woman had taken unlikely trouble to re-dress me again afterwards – as I awoke lying fully clothed on top of the covers, with the woman beside me, quite naked beneath them.

I quickly noticed something strange about the room (which was appropriate, as there was something extremely strange about my head), and soon realised that we were in a cabin on board a boat. It was the sound of the sea slapping outside which gave me my certainty, that and the fact I could see a small curtain which undoubtedly hid a brass porthole and not a wooden window. I did not know a motor boat could be so luxurious – nor did I know quite what to do. I think I dozed again for a while, till eventually the woman awoke and we smiled as we formally introduced ourselves.

Her name is Giselle de Froissard. It seems that we were definitely introduced formally to each other the previous evening, but neither of us could recall much of the incident. I apologised at once for my state, but she said that if a man was not permitted to get drunk on his birthday, then when could he get drunk? Apparently Giselle and her friends (who share this boat) took pity on me and, as no-one knew where I was staying, there seemed to be nowhere else to take me but their boat, and once on board the only vacant place apart from the floor was Giselle's double bed.

Having had breakfast of dark bread, coffee and the pulp of an orange, I was invited to join them on a trip they were making that day to one of the smaller bays along the rocky coast, where they would probably anchor overnight. Much as I wished to go with them and pursue the paths along which chance was taking me, I felt I had to decline as I was not good company and was in no state to enjoy anything, especially if the sun proved bright or the sea proved to be in any way choppy. Giselle understood, and we have arranged to meet again at the club this evening, where I had better clarify a remark she made to me as I left: 'Don't forget to think about Crete.'

This comment has fixed in my mind, but I am unable to dislodge any response from the jumble that is in there.

11 May

I am writing this entry as I sit on the deck of Alain's boat basking in the sun on my way to Crete. Alain is at the wheel Ferdinand is in theory navigating but somehow the map has found its way over his face and he now emits a gentle snore. Their two wives and Giselle are lying before me on the hot wooden deck, face up into the sun, quite naked and without embarrassment, and all three are becomingly brown all over. What a group of people! They evidently believe in *hédoné*, enjoying life to the full, and equally evidently have the money which enables them to do this. It seems that when they heard that I was travelling in Greece for the summer, they invited me to join them on their journey to the 'Great Island', and I had said nonchalantly that I might like to do that – hence Giselle's remark to me as I left.

She has just turned over and looked up to ask me if I am drawing them, and I said 'Drawing in words, perhaps – just a journal.' All three are now lying face down, presenting me with a delightful side view of three taut bottoms along the deck, the furthest almost at the edge of the deck and depending on the roll of the boat, outlined against the deep blue sea or the lighter shade of the sky. Not that it is a choppy ride; the sea is undulating gently, the weather is glorious and, I gather, unusually hot for the season.

Alain has thriving business interests in France, about which he seems deliberately vague, but which allow him to come away for a couple of months at a time and indulge his passion – this boat – and what better place could there be to indulge such a passion, or indeed any others.

Ferdinand, or 'Ferdie', works for Alain in some equally vague capacity while Jeanne and Coco, their wives, come along and revel in a life of laziness and spending. Giselle is a friend of Alain's, married but living apart from her husband, who is presently looking after their children. It seems that he was once a close colleague of Alain and Ferdie, but after an argument left whatever business it is that they had – I do not enquire too closely. After all, I am accepting their hospitality – they will not accept a shilling from me for the food they provide, though I did bring aboard two cases of resined wine for the journey, a gesture which I think was appreciated. Not that I imagine the bottles will last too long – their capacity for alcohol is formidable. I am trying to have a rather more sober time of it at the moment after my recent headache but, at the end of a meal with these people, their table resembles a bottle factory.

Giselle tells me slyly to put away my journal and join her – I say in a moment.

I had hoped that Giselle would not be expecting me to remove my bathing costume when I eventually joined the sun worshippers, but she and the other women insisted, though I have not yet seen Alain or Ferdie joining in this display. I did not like revealing the scar across my thigh, but my first worry was of burning from the sun – all very well for the women, who already have a deep colour over every visible inch, and for whom the sun merely turns them an even darker shade of brown. My own, how can I describe them, more private regions, are white as a new shirt, and if there is one part of me which I do not wish to be burned by the sun I know full well which part that is, so I insisted that it should only be for a short while so that my skin should have a fair chance to become accustomed to the sun.

My second worry became rather more major as I removed my costume and lay down between Giselle and Jeanne.

While watching the women earlier I had naturally enjoyed the sight of their firm bodies, but the stimulation remained a mental matter. Why my shaft should decide to become erect at the moment I myself became naked, I do not know. These days the wretched beast has a life of its own, I am convinced, and a malicious sense of humour too. I flopped quickly down on my stomach, and spent an uncomfortable few minutes pressed against the overhot deck while attempting to squirm surreptitiously so as to ease the unfortunate position in which I had lain. All this I tried to do, without arousing the attentions of the three women.

Giselle must have realised my discomfort, for she smiled slightly and glanced pointedly at me with her dark eyes, while Coco and Jeanne dozed and everything was blissfully calm all around us. Suddenly, Giselle moved to lie on her side, resting on her elbow, her substantial breasts scarcely a couple of feet from my face. How a woman so petite can have breasts so sizeable is beyond my comprehension – evidently anything is possible.

And what a delightful sight those firm breasts made in motion, as they rippled and gently bounced with the sway of the boat. They are as delightful to observe as they would be to caress, and Giselle was well aware of this. She began to rub my arm gently as we spoke, and to stroke my shoulder.

'Your back will be getting burned if you do not turn over soon,' she whispered, 'or per'aps you are shy?'

Thinking that perhaps after all she did not realise my predicament, I shifted my position and turned to lie on my side, facing her briefly, so no-one else would see. I was so hard I felt I was as close to her face as her breasts had been to mine. Giselle pursed her lips slightly and said with a wicked smile 'I get something in my eye?' And she pretended to rub her eye socket.

I turned onto my front again, but then a towel landed across my backside and I saw that Giselle was standing, wrapping a blue towel around herself.

'Come,' she said, 'I 'ave a something in my cabin which will cure the swelling.'

Rather shamefacedly, I followed after her determined stride as she marched past the captain and his snoozing navigator, down the brief run of steps to her cabin. No-one seemed the least bit concerned at our departure.

'We cannot 'ave this,' she insisted in her delightful French accent, as she leaned back on the closed door. 'You had better lie on the bed. Coco and Jeanne will be getting jealous if they see you like that, and then Alain will get angry.' I lay on my back on her bed, and I stared at Giselle as my penis stared at the ceiling. She dropped her towel to the floor and came over to me, squeezing my hardness so tightly it almost hurt. To my surprise she immediately knelt astride me, over my hips, still holding my shaft and stroked herself between the legs with the tip so that I could feel her opening lips. She pushed and I slid deep into her with satisfying fullness, and gave out a groan of pleasure as I filled Giselle, feeling totally consumed by her.

Giselle leaned forward and swayed her large breasts before me, enabling me to push up on my elbows and reach them, sucking her brown skin and tugging her nipples so that they grew to taut deep brown buds. All the while, Giselle was swaying very slowly back and forth, her fingers feeling me moving in and out of her, and then she sat up away from me, and I raised my knees to support her back as she arched herself. Her fingers were no longer gripping me but were touching herself, and I knew she was rubbing the tiny mound that gives women their pleasure. I moved her fingers aside and rubbed against her damp flesh with my thumb, enjoying the sight of my shaft burying inside her, taken to the hilt, to emerge again with a delicious thrill as it almost came completely out, her wet lips just holding it by the head.

Giselle was making all kinds of sound by this time, the positions of our bodies obviously giving her immense pleasure. For me it was more of a slow build to pleasure rather than the quickening passion of thrusting into a woman from on top or behind. We must try it in that way again.

Giselle would lean forward for a time as I licked her swollen nipples then lean back again, rubbing my penis with her fingers, but it was when she arched backwards that she received most satisfaction and it was in that position, when both my hands gripped her breasts, that she gave a series of quick groans then fell forward and looked at me with a serious face, almost speechless and lost, saying 'Now . . . now . . .' and I held her tight by her round hips and thrust myself up into her as she pushed down, again and again and as hard and as fast as I could till I climaxed with a long shuddering moan, and she let out a squeal and collapsed forwards sweating against me.

What a joy to discover new ways of pleasing and of being pleased. We were both lost for a few minutes in our respective pleasure, then we emerged and kissed each other many times on shoulder and face. Giselle eased her legs from her crouching position around my waist and lay full-length on top of me, till my penis, limp now, eased out in a satisfied slide.

'A good cure?' Giselle asked.

14 May

We are harboured in Hania, a beautiful old town in northern Crete, where the buildings show their mixture of influences, mediaeval or ancient, of Venetian, Byzantine, Greek, and more recently Turkish. There is still a mosque on one side of the harbour, the first I have seen in Greece, and many Turks still live here, outnumbering the Greeks in many districts, reinforcing the feeling that the island has not long been a part of Greece.

It almost grieves me now to be so happy. No, not the happiness itself, but the knowledge that such happiness is possible when I have lived a life of such misery and fear for the past few years. Not that I would regret fighting for a just cause – but what cause? An obscure sequence of events and political wrangling at the opposite end of Europe, and for that millions of Englishmen, Frenchmen, Germans and Austrians are to lay down their lives? I shall take my pleasures now with a vengeance – no government will claim me for its pile of dead bodies. And yet with my scar and my limp how close I came to that pile.

I am thankful for my survival, and hope that from now I will make my own decisions. I intend to do whatever I wish to do, in order to make my life happy. I am secretly pleased that when it came to the test I had the strength to join the ranks of ordinary soldiers, rather than accept the commission that was offered me. Yet it seems one cannot reject the past – it is always around one's neck, like it or not, because other people hang it there, and it can no more be shaken off than a poor man can freely shake off his poverty.

What a curious thing a diary is – truly a reflection of thought, mirroring obliquely its moods and obsessions, its worries and changes, day by day.

16 May

We have sailed along the coast, passed the fishing port of Rethymnon, once a Venetian capital, to Crete's main town – city almost – Heraklion, a port which is a little grubby, none too pleasant to my eyes, but a change of scene and certainly with plenty of life. The French people know Heraklion's nightlife, having been here before, but this is all new and rather surprising to me. Indeed the whole of the last few days has been that – I have never lived aboard a large motor boat before, and have never encountered people as sophisticated as Giselle and her friends. I could never imagine 'English' people behaving in such a manner – indeed, I am surprised to find myself doing so – yet it seems very natural, their walking naked around the boat, accepting that Giselle will take a young lover such as myself – for I have no illusions about what I am to her, nor what she is to me.

We are enjoying each other's company and each other's

bodies for the moment . . . and in time she will return home to her luxuried life in France, while I will continue my wandering. We know our affair has no future, but is that any reason to deny the pleasure we both derive from it? Should we both sit around all day at our separate tables, and sleep at night in our separate beds, when briefly we could be much happier together? And besides, it is a great pleasure to indulge in love-making without a sheath, for Giselle has told me that she can have no more children. No, enjoy whatever may come your way, that is now my belief!

18 May

Yesterday we went east from Heraklion, round a headland into a large sheltered bay, and moored for lunch at a simple village named for St Nicholas. It is somewhere near here that Zeus was born. There were a few white-washed tavernas, and one of these was able to provide us with a bean stew, tomatoes, bread, olives and olive oil and, of course, more wine. We were immediately objects of great curiosity, and I wished I could hear properly what the groups of men at the various surrounding tables had to say about us all.

Several of the villagers, I noticed, had hands missing, with their arms ending in stumps, the result of using dynamite for fishing. Apparently, this stuns the fish for a long way around the explosion and results in a much greater and easier catch than using a net, although a few of the older men say it exhausts the waters. The throwing of dynamite has to be timed correctly, as it must not explode in mid-air, too far from the water, nor must it hit the water with too great a length of fuse still to burn, and risk being extinguished. The loss of a hand invariably results from a moment's bad timing. All this I learn from Alain.

When lunch had had time to settle, we moved on to find an empty beach in which to laze the afternoon away – there are no shortages of such beaches along this stretch of the coast, and all empty as the Greeks themselves seem to have no interest in swimming for the sake of it, the only companions you find being the occasional ragged flock of sheep or goats. These beaches tend not to be the most attractive for lying on!

Behind the beach we chose was a rough twisting path, and as I had become restless I announced that I would like to stretch my legs and take a walk along it. To my surprise Giselle wanted to come – surprised because, although fit, Giselle is not outwardly the most energetic of people, at least not in that respect. The path first wound through scrubland behind the beach, with more evidence of goats on the way, then up the gentle side of a small hill until it reached a headland overlooking our beach. From here we could see along the coast in both directions and also see behind us, a long way inland, the huge purple mountains of central Crete rising in the distance.

Below us lay the sleeping shapes of the others; apart from this we were alone in the space and the silence. I put my arm around Giselle, enjoying the peace, and she nestled her head against my shoulder. There are no words for that feeling of serenity.

The moment led to a great desire in me to take Giselle, and when I looked into her watching eyes I knew she wanted the same. Our first gentle kiss turned quickly into something more passionate, and then we were burned by lust, in contrast to the quiet moment before. It was a violent love-making. We moved back into the scrub slightly so that we would not be visible to those on the beach, and then I stripped off Giselle's grey bathing costume and then my own, so that we stood stark naked on the headland, two figures in the ancient landscape.

I bent my knees slightly, so that I could thrust my erection in between Giselle's open legs and feel the damp of her full lips and the scrape of her curling hair against the head of my aching penis. I remembered briefly that time with Agnes, but there were no half-hearted erections on this occasion – and no nonsense about making love standing up, either.

Giselle sank to her knees before me, and took my shaft deep into her mouth for a few moments, lovingly sucking and kissing me, then she pulled me down to the dry earth. As Giselle lay there on her back waiting, I pushed her knees apart, needing to sink myself right into her, but not before I had gazed at the beautiful sight of her swollen moist lips lying open to me. Giselle held me and pulled me into her, and I groaned at that delicious pleasure of sliding into her till I filled her body completely.

In my lust I plunged swiftly back and forth within her, and pushed deep with no thought for delay or her pleasure. I desperately wanted to ram myself into her damp body again and again until I burst inside her and then Giselle was pleading, 'Yes, yes,' and demanding 'do it, do it.'

Amid the scrub and wild vines under that blue sky with the burning sun on my back, and with my arms pushing and scratching against the dry earth, the act felt so primitive that I shuddered quickly and collapsed onto Giselle, both of us sweating and gasping as if we could melt into each other and be fused together there in the sparse landscape for ever.

In time I asked Giselle if she had climaxed and she said no but that she was satisfied. She described it as a kind of small climax, a gush of warmth and pleasure as my seed burst into her and flooded her. She told me that this is sometimes all a woman wants, a different kind of satisfaction. The simple act of love is all but simple, with as many variations as a symphony.

Later we washed away our heat and sweat in the warm sea, and last night slept together with no need for sex.

20 May

Still moored in Heraklion, and so busily indulging life to the full that I find little time or circumstance to write. Privacy is essential, as otherwise all will want to know what I am writing, and I feel I could not write openly with the knowledge that someone might suddenly lean over my shoulder and read this page.

Privacy on a boat, and in the way of life we are all leading at the moment is rather hard to find, even on a boat as large as this. But today I am suffering from a slight stomach upset and the others have gone ashore to stock up on food and, more importantly to them, on drink. They are planning to have lunch there, too, so I will have the boat to myself for some hours – a blessed relief. Although really I am enjoying this stay with Giselle, it is still good to have time to myself occasionally.

Most days we wake surprisingly early, considering the lateness of some of the nights, but the bright sun soon revives everyone. It is a lovely feeling to wake up next to a beautiful and naked woman, to feel our legs knotted together or to reach out and touch her, or feel her reach out to me and place her arm about me. We like to lie so, drowsing, with my thigh pressed between her legs. Sometimes we make love, and sometimes not, but in either case the feeling is of love of the undemanding companionable sort.

I help now on the boat a little, getting her ready to sail. And we often take the boat out and along the coast to find another secluded bay where we can pull in, to bathe and picnic. It is my first experience (among so many first experiences!) of swimming naked in the warm and salty sea – a wonderful, clean feeling of freedom, uninhibited and unrestricted by a bathing suit, as if one were an animal and belonged to the ocean. Sometimes it is hard not to be aroused, with three beautiful women swimming naked beside me, or lying sunning themselves on the beach a few yards from my gaze; and yet at other times it all seems surprisingly innocent, as if we were children with no knowledge of shame.

We all take great care not to offend other people, and

always choose beaches that are either so secluded as to be only accessible by boat, or backed by a large sweeping bay where we could see anyone in the distance long before they arrived; not that anyone as yet has interrupted our idylls, for the wild northern coast here is wonderfully long and deserted. Dark, rugged and wind-haunted mountains rise in the background, running in spikes down the spine of the island. The foothills and valleys are dense with a thick growth of deep green – full of life, which is my own feeling as I float naked in the salt sea and look back at this harsh and beautiful land. It is for me as if Greece is become that biblical Garden, and I am beginning to wonder how I will ever be able to leave. Although September is still some way off, it is nevertheless slowly approaching.

I really am starting to think that I would like this trip to continue on into the winter. How can even Oxford compare with the way I am living now, the freedom I have? How can what I learn there compare with what I am learning now, being here, learning about myself from the people I meet? I am fascinated by the so different lives that people lead, fascinated to know that a group of people like Alain's live the lives that they do. How can I know the fullness or emptiness of my own life unless I have a number of others, sufficiently different, with which to compare it? In France I learned a great deal about one narrow area, and yet somehow I am only now coming to understand the limitations of what I learned.

Giselle teaches me just by living the way she lives – she enjoys a life of total indulgence, of serious pleasure, and while I have learnt that pleasure is to be enjoyed, I could never adopt that kind of life – briefly, yes, but not for ever.

I wish too much to learn, to see other things. I want to visit the ancient ruins of the Palace at Knossos that are now so famous, yet no-one from the group shows any interest when I suggest it. At least it would take them away from their sand and water. I thought perhaps Giselle might wish to come with me, but she said she would be bored. At least she is honest, but it would have been pleasant if she had been able to say that she would accompany me because I wished to go. I also wish to go, quite simply, so that I can describe them in detail to father, and reassure him that his allowance to me for this summer is being well spent. If only he knew what sights rather than sites I have been seeing of late.

22 May

Indeed, the break was not long in arriving. A sad moment, yet a necessary one. Alain was ready to move on, to take his boat and travel on around the island, discovering new anchorages and coves in which to bathe. To accompany them was a tempting thought. The more so for being linked in my mind with continuing to discover Giselle, but it was not tempting enough and I wished now to continue to discover Crete and the rest of Greece for myself, and not to spend every day in the same manner, which might then seem to me on reflection to be something of a waste when I return to England in the autumn. Still, it was strange to wake up in a strange room this morning, not only ashore but alone.

23 May

Having made my break from the group, and I do miss their humour and hunger for life, I felt I had to do what I had wanted to do, which was make the journey to Knossos. It was only about three miles distant from where I had taken a room, not a long walk, but because the sun is soon so very high and hot in the sky, I left after breakfast at eight o'clock to ensure that I would not still be trudging when the sun began to burn. Once again I was surprised by how quickly one can leave the outskirts of such a large town behind, and be out in the olive green of the countryside, lined with pale stone walls and echoing with bird song, the warm air scented by a hundred delicious flowers and herbs, none of which I am capable of identifying. I do wish I knew what they were, yet all I can say is that on the way there were small purple flowers and larger yellow ones – fields almost full of vivid blood red poppies.

The rough road winds round in such a way that three miles as the crow flies must easily be six as a man walks – but a pleasant walk along an undemanding road down in a valley, accompanied for much of the way by a shallow stream that was struggling for survival. A stream that will surely be a moist ditch then a dry gully before the summer is at its height.

As the hills grew higher and more rugged on either side, I reached what I assume from my guide book to be the villa described as belonging to Evans himself, set in a beautiful and no doubt bountiful vineyard, the leaves full, the grapes themselves seeming almost ready to be picked. Restricting myself instead to a mouthful of water from a leather bag I bought in Heraklion, I rested awhile on the low wall outside (the villa seems now deserted) before continuing a little further, to be confronted on turning a corner by the site of the ruins themselves. Scattered among the low walls and shallow trenches were students, digging in small intent groups, and I could not help but recall Anna and the site at Delphi, and how much more such sites meant when explained by someone who knew and understood.

I do admit to glancing round at some of the young women who were working on the site, checking if Anna was among them, but she was not and it was rather an unlikely prospect.

Perhaps I should have stayed in Delphi a little longer, instead of hastening to leave. Maybe I could have healed the rift between us. Yet if I had done that, other events would not have happened. Sometimes life seems confused and full of *chaos*, truly a Greek work, at other times it seems to have a ruthless logic that moves it harshly on to inevitable developments and conclusions. Perhaps it is both, simultaneously, and our viewpoint merely changes.

I walked slowly around Knossos, trying to piece together limited and, no doubt by now, out-dated information from the guide. And despite my lack of real knowledge I could still see and understand enough to be sufficiently impressed. I stood for a while looking into a pit, where two young men were busy attending to something in the ground – not digging it out exactly, but brushing off dust and slowly scraping away dry soil to reveal a rather drab-looking mosaic beneath.

An elderly man in shorts came and stood beside me, and addressed me gruffly in English: 'You realise we are privileged to be the first people to look upon that mosaic for maybe four thousand years?'

Drab mosaic or not, the simple truth of that statement, which I had not been considering, made the moment magical. As if reading my mind, he went on to tell me that the mosaic might look dull and uninteresting, but I should try to imagine it in the full glory of its ancient reds and blues and greens and bright whites.

'Imagine setting foot on that,' he said. 'Quite beautiful.'

With that, he wandered off rather unsteadily, leaving a memory of boyish enthusiasm still evident in his old eyes. I wondered how he knew I was English, unless he was one of those Englishmen who assume that everyone speaks their language. Or perhaps he had spied the guide book I was carrying.

I spent several hours exploring the site, asking some of the workers what it was they were doing, and listening to the halting answers – they were a mixed group of nationalities, but many spoke either a little English or, like me, some primitive Greek. No Danish students among them, though, and no women as pretty as Anna or her friends. Perhaps I should try my luck at Epidavros! Why not attempt to mix culture with pleasure?

25 May

I have been thinking that I *will* go to Epidavros after all. If nothing else, at least if I plan ahead I can send my parents a *poste restante* address. Knowing my mother's delight at sending out letters in virtually every post, there must by now be stacks of mail for me dotted about half the towns in Greece. These days she probably sends them out to places at random, in the hope that I might turn up there and find a letter waiting! I shall send them both another picture postcard from Knossos, they will like that. And I must write, too, to describe in detail my wanderings – though perhaps I will not go too deep into Giselle and the naked bathing (and other pursuits). I will also send a letter as soon as I can and tell them to write to me at Epidavros, as I am now making plans to go there in the next week or so.

27 May

Now I shall have to write to them again, for in doing a little reading I have discovered that there is no actual town at Epidavros. It is just a site containing the ancient ruins, so goodness knows where letters addressed to the Epidavros *poste restante* will find themselves.

The place nearest Epidavros where I can stay, and which is large enough to have a proper post office, would appear from my guide to be Naplion (muddlingly called Naflion or even Nauplion, in some maps), so they will have to write to me there. There must also surely be a bank at Naplion and by the time I arrive I think I will almost be ready to send for more money from Athens. I spent very little while with Giselle – Alain was a very generous host, though I never was able to discover the source of his money. Perhaps better to imagine something dramatic like gun-running or smuggling. The truth is that he probably owned factories that made sausages or surgical appliances, just as ours make and bottle preserve, and that is why he remained quiet about it.

1 June

Reaching Epidavros is not going to be as straightforward as I thought. Henry's Law applies. It seems that when one wants to go nowhere, every Greek port has a dozen boats going to almost every other Greek port, yet as soon as one has somewhere particular for which to aim, there are immediately no boats going in that direction for weeks, unless I take an extremely circuitous route *via* thirteen different islands, at least half of them in quite the wrong direction from where I am headed. It seems that I could go to Rhodes – but for that I would require a pass in triplicate of some kind from the local Italian consul, who is probably the kind of official who makes even the Greek civil servants look efficient – from Rhodes I am assured there will be a

A.N.A.D.—6

boat, via several more islands, to an island called Poros; from here I can cross to the mainland and catch a bus to Naplion and Epidavros. This is the easiest route!

No, I exaggerate, it would be quite possible to catch a steamer direct to Athens, then a boat or bus or train to take me to Naplion, but returning to Athens on a lengthy and, in my present state, expensive steamer trip does not appeal. I am told in a café at the port that if I am prepared to wait, there may be someone crossing to the mainland direct. I asked the man who told me this what this depended on, and the answer was a lip-curling shrug. He told me to try Hania, so tomorrow I shall make the trip back there – it was a pretty town, and I should be glad to revisit it.

2 June

In Hania, at the harbourside, I have dined in style on some freshly killed fish. It was a little disconcerting to be taken into the small kitchen and shown fish swimming in a salt-water tank and asked to pick out the one I wanted. However, as the tank was heavily crowded I eased my guilt by telling myself that any fish I chose would be glad to be out of it, and the others would have a little more room!

No luck with the boats yet, but I will continue to walk around the port and make acquaintances – my man back in Itea warned me of that. It seems that many of the captains would rather not talk too loudly about their destinations, and until they know that you are not on a mission from the authorities they may even deny that they ever intend to go anywhere. This makes very good sense. Imagine that you were planning a clandestine trip to a secret destination and a stranger walked up and asked if you know of a boat going to that very place. What are you to think? To deny it would be the obvious reaction.

I have spent a pleasant evening, with a meal that was as good as it was cheap, and as I now drink my coffee and watch the lights of the harbour bobbing like tiny lightboats on the black oily surface of the water, I think that there can be no finer place to be. Once again, the prospect of staying in this country for ever takes on an attractive glow – though perhaps only through the golden haze of straw-coloured wine.

4 June

I decided on a walk today, west on the road out of Hania, and then turned along a rough track that ran inland towards the lower slopes of the lovely green-grey hills which surround here. One of the unexpected beauties of Hania for me is the way that on turning a street corner there suddenly, framed by the houses on either side, is a view of the distant hills at the end of the street.

As I walked further inland I came upon a woman, painting at an easel at the far edge of an olive grove. Curiosity overcame me, and because she was so engrossed in her work I called out '*Yassoo*', a Greek greeting, so as not to frighten her as I approached.

She immediately turned her head, on which a large and floppy straw hat topped her red hair, and returned the greeting, although in an accent that was unmistakably American, yet still quiet and restrained. I apologised at once for intruding, saying that it must be awful as an artist to have someone for ever looking over her shoulder or disrupting her work, but she said, out of politeness, that she didn't mind too much. We exchanged a few pleasantries, and I discovered that she was staying at a hotel in Hania. When I said I was surprised not to have seen her, she told me, with a slight smile, that she was out painting flowers all day, and did not venture far from her room in the evening. So I have persuaded her – against her judgement, I feel – to dine with me tonight at one of the harbour restaurants.

5 June

I am sitting beside Amy in a large field, enjoying the sun while she concentrates on capturing the outline in pencil of a vivid yellow flower (I must ask her again what it is, for I have already forgotten). I say she has probably come a month too late to see the best of the blooms, many of which have now gone, but she is here on commission, at the request of an American publisher to prepare illustrations for a book on Mediterranean plant life. She says they did not trouble over such matters as what might be the right time to come – vaguely in the spring or early summer was good enough.

Amy has been here in Greece for a few weeks, travelling around much as I have done. She made her way to Crete in search of a few species unique to the island. It is a joy to have someone to talk to, and from whom I can learn a little about the flora, their names, and their relations. Amy has shown me some of her work, in pencil and watercolours, and it seems astonishingly good to my eyes. The first requisite is botanical accuracy, of course, but she has tried to bring some sense of movement and of setting into her paintings, and the result is a strong feeling of life.

We talked last night about each other, as strangers do, and enjoyed ourselves though always with a certain restraint. It seemed to me as if she were holding something back – that she smiled where others might have laughed; but she was not averse to my offer to accompany her on her walk today, as long as I promised not to look over her shoulder – which is why I am sitting at a distance from her, enjoying the sun, and trying to write a verse about being in Greece, seemingly outside of time. Which I must now return to, having broken off concentration for a few minutes to jot down these lines.

9 June

I feel a little ashamed of myself, a little confused. I have been enjoying the last few days with Amy, quiet days and evenings of good conversation as we learn a little about each other and each other's countries and ways of life. Yet part of that enjoyment, for me, has been the thought that perhaps here is another 'conquest' – for Amy is certainly attractive, with a short, fashionable almost boyish crop of rust-coloured hair, and although petite in face and body, is neatly shaped and perhaps eight or so inches shorter than my own thin six-foot. Very appealing, but because there is this 'something' reticent about her, I have not even attempted to touch her arm, being sure that she requires a slower and far more gentle approach.

And now – while I have frequently been trying to imagine her without clothes, in the passionate throes of making love – I have at last discovered what it is she has been holding back, and I feel awful that my main thought towards her was of my own possible sexual enjoyment. As we were dining last night, I made a glib remark I have made before, that I was surprised an attractive woman like her had never married. (She had already told me that she had never met the right man.) She stopped me then and said quietly that it wasn't true when she said she had never married, but it was something about which she found it difficult to talk and so it was safer to stay clear of the subject.

Her husband was killed in a dreadful railway accident almost a year ago, and this is her first visit away from home on her own – they had travelled much together in America and were planning to visit Europe when the war was over, but now here she was on her own, and missing him terribly.

The work she is doing was given her by a publishing friend, to try to help her resume both a career given up when she married, and her independent life, and to bring her out and away from her home (their home) and travelling and rediscovering life. She says she knows that she has to do this, but that, all the same, it is not an easy thing to do.

After this revelation I feel, as I say, ashamed that I have been thinking of her only in a selfish way, as another woman to enjoy – yet not totally like that, surely. I genuinely like her for her company, and my sole desire has not been to take her and then move on. As we walked home along the darkened streets and I said goodnight outside the lamp-lit entrance to her hotel, she took my hand, squeezed it and said, quite simply, 'Thank you.' Then she was gone.

11 June

Not half an hour ago, while we were starting to enjoy our picnic of coarse bread and goat's cheese, Amy said the strangest thing to me. More than ever I am learning the complicated nature of people's feelings, and of their needs and their ways of showing or not showing emotion, but this surprised me quite. I had imagined, following her words the night before last, that our friendship would continue in its platonic way until the end of this week when she left to return to America.

Perhaps it still will, for I do not know what to make of her strange request, that we should spend the night together without becoming lovers. I did hesitate, as various conflicting thoughts criss-crossed like electricity through my mind – that a night with Amy would delight me, no doubt, and perhaps when the moment came she would want more. Then I wondered if in agreeing I would not be taking advantage of her own evident uncertainty, and whether it would not be better to keep such relationship we had on a purely friendly basis; for to spend a night together could be the wrong thing to do.

These and other thoughts ran wildly through my head in a fraction of a second, and when I did not immediately answer Amy said, 'Of course you may not want to . . .'

And to this I could only say, 'No, it's not that . . .' And from there the consequence seemed inevitable. We continue to eat our bread and cheese, and drink our retsina, in the sun and a silence broken only by quiet smiles.

12 June

As my room is more of a side-street lodging house, and the unlit entrance has a certain amount of privacy, last night Amy came back with me after our meal at the harbourside rather than face me trying to sneak into her hotel.

She said repeatedly that she was not really sure why she was doing this but that she wanted to; to share a bed again, and that it seemed right to do this now. Her fears and the loneliness of an empty bed weigh on her, who has been used for so long to its being shared. I told her gently to stop talking, at which she smiled and blew out the small lamp, saying that she preferred to undress in the dark.

We both undressed, without haste, and although I have taken to sleeping naked because of the heat, Amy was wearing a thin nightgown that she must have packed in her handbag. We rather nervously folded our arms around one another, and then she placed her head against my neck so that I was able to rub my cheek slowly against her hair and inhale its sweet perfume. With that arousing scent and the feel of her soft body against mine through the thin cotton of her gown, I soon felt my shaft harden and grow, although I swear in truth I did not want that to happen, lest Amy be offended or form the wrong opinion as to my purpose in agreeing to her request. But I need not have worried.

Her leg was resting over me and she could not help but feel my arousal against her thigh, yet all that happened was she shifted a little to take my firmness gently in her hand and told me that it was good to know she could still have that effect on a man. Then she kissed me again at the side of the neck, softly but with such deep warmth of feeling that the moment, with her fingers firmly around me and her body against me, was at the same time both profoundly innocent and profoundly erotic. Holding each other in that manner, we slept.

13 June

Such innocence could not continue, and last night when we climbed into bed together a second time and put our arms about each other in the darkness again, I grew once more and she held me again, but still more tightly this time, and moved her hand back and forth along me, pushing the skin and filling my body with excitement and anticipation.

Gently, I stroked her shoulders through the thin nightgown, and then the soft skin of her arms; and finding her face in the darkness I kissed her lips. She responded, but slightly, in tenderness rather than in passion; and in tenderness I responded too, obeying her request not to speak, but using my lips instead to kiss as much of her bare neck and shoulders as the nightgown would allow. I brushed my fingers over her breasts through the material, almost flat as she lay on her back, yet I could feel the nipples rising quite large, so I reached down and gently tugged up her gown till it rucked above her waist and I could slide my fingers under it to caress those breasts and feel the nipples harden under my fingers, teasing them to even greater tautness so they grew astonishingly and pressed against my palms. My elbow brushed the bush of curling hair that grew between her legs, and I pressed my arm against the hardness of her mound, feeling her push her hips upwards against me, rubbing her quim urgently against the bone of my arm.

Her legs parted slightly as she abandoned herself more to the moment, and I smoothed my fingers down her flat stomach into the bush of hair and along the opening quim that lay beneath, damp and delightful. The moist folds slithered against my inquisitive touch, as I found the tiny bud, the one inside. But as I pressed more firmly with my fingers Amy said 'No, gently.' My mouth was gentle as it moved slowly down her body and between her open legs, my tongue probing deep between her parted lips and up into her tight salty wetness.

'Now,' she insisted, and pulled my head up to kiss me deeply as I slid inside her. All thought of silence had gone now as she achingly insisted 'Yes, Now, Please.' and gave a shuddering moan of pleasure long before I myself was ready to spurt into her.

I continued to thrust my shaft into her, my whole body tensing as my own moment of climax approached, and again Amy started to moan, tightening around me, and after a brief time came that long and abandoned moan, as of a soul lost in a pit of pleasure. Only then did my own moment arrive and, as it did, she raised her open legs and wrapped them tightly around my back, so that I was trapped firmly inside her just as I thrust in and shuddered. The feeling was so intense that my breath came in shuddering gasps and stars were wheeling in my head. It was truly the most intense moment of pleasure I have ever felt, and it was followed by the warmest, most relaxed feeling as Amy held me closely to her. I made her happy, she said. I assured her that she did the same for me, as I wrapped her small body in my arms, and we whispered ourselves to sleep.

16 June

All still goes well between Amy and myself, shadowed slightly by the fact that she must take the ferry to Athens in two days, from where she will return to New York. Because she confided in me, and because I feel sure we will never again meet (despite promises to write and to see each other) I have talked to her in some detail about both my past experiences, and my present confusion. Yesterday, by mid-day, she had finished the last of the necessary illustrations and we returned to her smart hotel room after our usual picnic lunch – though I'd taken along a particularly good local wine to help celebrate the end of her work. Strange how no-one in the hotel turns a hair if I visit Amy's room during the day, yet no visitors are allowed late at night! As if the day could only be for the most innocent of activities – though, in my view, our activities yesterday afternoon *were* quite innocent, and why two people making each other gloriously happy in this manner should be frowned upon, if mentioned at all, is something I shall never be able to understand!

However, after our afternoon's love, we lay naked in the bright bands of sunlight that sliced through the green painted shutters, and talked in low voices – murmurs so low as if to bypass speech and ensure that thoughts went straight from heart to heart. Amy had told me that she decided when her husband died that she would not love another man, as that would be betrayal of what she felt for him. We do not profess to love each other, on such short acquaintance, but she says that through these days with me, she feels the possibility of love, of pleasure and kindnesses. There is, I think, no betrayal, for every love must be different, so no honest comparisons can be made; and a new love now does not deny an earlier love that already and so for ever exists.

'What of you,' she asked me quietly, 'your loves,' and I told her that I had not had many. I wanted to be truthful, yet to say that I have only loved four women, and all within the past few months, would spoil the bond that has grown between us. Therefore I said instead that I had not yet truly loved one woman, though I had experienced a few small romances. This is true, in its fashion. My only sin being one of omission, in not stating when these small romances occurred.

From that, and against my will, talk drifted to the war that has just passed. Amy ran her fingers along my scar and wanted to know the truth. How awful was it? What did it do to a man?

I told her I had enlisted as a common soldier, against my family's wishes. It offended them, but if I was going to fight I did not want that accident of birth to give me what I thought to be the more comfortable task.

I learned, though, and quickly, that there were no easy jobs in that nightmare. Only those at the top, not those at the front, would survive. If I was to fight, I had decided I would fight as an equal among fellow men.

I told Amy something of the conditions of war, though no telling can convey the blind horror, the squalor, or the cold, the misery and the degradation when one ceases to have the least scrap of self respect, when one looks at the boots rotting on one's feet, and wonders where flesh ends and leather begins, when one picks the lice from one's hair, without emotion or shame. Our minds and sensibilities were dead. And then one day someone would perform a similar act, no better or worse than a hundred other acts, and what we were, and what we were doing suddenly struck through the deadened senses like lightning.

Of the fighting, nothing could be less like one imagined. Precious little excitement, daring, bravery, no constant whine of shells nor thud of guns. For day after day we would sit around, digging new trenches, repairing old ones, watching, waiting, doing anything necessary to relieve the boredom (for there is not a great deal of recreational opportunity in a trench). Often we had little idea of exactly where we were, though place names could occasionally be found if one took the trouble to look. No one deemed it necessary to tell us where we actually were, where it was we might be dying on the 'morrow. Nor did anyone feel it important, these staff officers I was so encouraged to join, to tell the men the purpose of what they were doing. Two days of inactivity would go by, then without explanation some staff captain, visiting only, would come along the trench and say that tomorrow at dawn we were all going over the top and taking that hill directly to the north. Information was limited to a brief 'Quite heavily defended' or 'Shouldn't offer any resistance,' though no reliance could be put on these statements, as they were more often than not wildly inaccurate.

This lack of information was, for me at least, one of the worst aspects of the whole affair. Even on the sunniest days, I felt I was still fighting in the dark. It would have helped if someone had simply taken ten minutes to explain that we were taking that hill because we needed to push the line forward at this point; it being known that German support was weak there.

Knowing that others would be doing the same elsewhere, each unit reliant on the other, would have encouraged everyone greatly. Yet not a glimmer of this information came to lighten our darkness.

These are virtually the very words I used to Amy yesterday, and she listened, and squeezed my arm from time to time in silent understanding. Though I have not yet told anyone the half of it. Can life ever be understood? My mind goes back to those miserable times, reliving them most closely, then I return to the present to gaze upon Amy's smooth and naked body lying beside me. I can imagine no more perfect place, no more beautiful sight than this, the glowing skin, the flowing lines, the grace in repose, the tension in passion. Yet we will not all be content to love life, to love love. We must go out to fight, to destroy landscapes, towns, villages, families . . . and bodies beautiful as this among them. Yet we are capable of giving and receiving such happiness.

18 June

Amy sailed early this morning for Athens, the boat leaving at 6 a.m., and I went along to help her with her travelling bags and to see her off. It was a sad and surprisingly touching moment. We had become so very intimate in such a short space of time, and I feel a bond has formed between us, because we have each learned so much of the other's life. Will I see her again? I would like to think so, and I have her address in America and she mine in England. Someone else to whom I promise to send picture postcards and the occasional letter!

The morning seems empty without her. By now she will

be half-way to Athens, and tonight on her own in a hotel in Piraeus. We agreed, on parting, that we would both retire to bed at exactly eleven o'clock, and lie still for a while and remember being in each other's arms. I liked Amy, and by such gestures memories are kept.

Last night it was not memory but reality. Because of the 5 o'clock start that we needed, we dined early at the side-street restaurant near the harbour and our meal was tinged with a peculiar air that seemed to be happy and sad at once. We both chose our favourite foods, in what had become our favourite place to eat, and I treated us to one of the more expensive Greek wines. We talked not of parting but of the memories we would keep of our short time together, and of the future; of the fierce beauty of Crete, and of our fondness for each other.

We no longer needed to be coy with one another. Last night in my sparse room we undressed together in the lamplight with no embarrassment, and stood naked and at ease in the warm night air. I told Amy that if I were a painter I could have painted her, naked, as she paints the flowers. Words are a poor substitute. Amy protested that she wished she had thought to make a portrait of me; but that she might, as a figure in a Greek landscape, from memory one day.

Talking done, we lay on the bed and I rested beside her, propped on one elbow looking down at her smooth naked body in the lamplight's warm glow. My fingers ran themselves through her short red hair, then brushed along the line of her neck, and down her body, between small breasts, softly over her trembling stomach and down to her waiting mound of hair to touch the dampness between her legs just momentarily. We kissed and she shivered as I moved my mouth to kiss her breasts, and gently suck her rising nipples, then her stomach, until my tongue reached just above where her black hairs began.

She parted her legs in invitation, and I moved to rest between her open thighs, where I played my tongue along her moist salt quim which opened and swelled under my touch.

I had to mouth her gently at first as she was always sensitive to touch, and the merest breath seemed to make her shudder and tremble. I teased her open lips with my tongue, running it slowly around her moist folds and occasionally pressing its hot enveloping wetness hard against her small taut button. My shaft was stiff and aching as I tickled and teased her in this manner, probing into her as she thrust her hips towards me till her breathing quickened, her sighing turned into groans, then the groans lengthened, became deeper, splitting into uncontrolled panting grunts as Amy threw her head from side to side on the pillow. She tumbled into the fullest pleasure with a shudder gripping my head with her knees, at the last using her hands to pull me from her.

It was some minutes before she was ready to take my rampant shaft into her and share her pleasure with me, but then I slipped deep inside her and her soft, moist walls closed tight around me, gripping me while I pumped my shaft into her, spurred on by her murmurs and whispers. I quickened my thrusts till I knew my spasm of pleasure was building to an ache, then I pushed rapidly into her like a machine and the joy was intense as I gushed and gushed, as if I would never stop spurting.

It makes me hard just writing. By tonight we will be many hours apart, and soon separated by the width of an ocean, yet nothing can split the togetherness we have felt. I wish her well.

16 July

I write this by flickering lamplight in the sparsely-furnished upstairs room of a small hotel overlooking the waterfront at Kavala. I have travelled to that curve of harsh mainland to the north of the Aegean, where the bare mountains rise out of the marshland of the coastal plain.

My thoughts this past month have not been for recording, though I have spent much of this time alone on ferries, moving on. Poems preoccupy me, mostly so bad that I throw them away with no consideration of attempting any further work.

Talk with Amy triggered unsettling thoughts – of the past and of the future in this land. I await a letter from father saying that he approves and has made the arrangements. I don't need, for my own sake, his formal approval, but if I am to stay another year here a continued remittance would be extremely helpful, or my own savings will dwindle to nothing. There is some casual work available, such as fruit-picking, but it is poorly paid – I have had several invitations to help with the coming autumn olive crops in places I have stayed, but they would scarcely provide me with more than food and lodging. To survive without an allowance, I would need a job such as a waiter or something along those lines, perhaps in Athens over the winter; but then problems of official papers would present themselves.

If it comes, father's allowance will be useful, even though it goes against everything I have felt about not accepting gifts of privilege, of being determined to make my own way in my own manner. His payments to me to cover the few brief months I was intended and was intending to spend here originally seemed to be a reasonable compromise between conscience and necessity, and it pleased him to send me away to complete my education before settling down to the academic life of Oxford. It has certainly done that.

I am become more selfish, however. My anger at those wasted years is only now being vented. In the immediate past little pieces of it are all that I have acknowledged. Of course I am angry, and bitter. I was forced to spend some of the most important years of my life in an army battling for a cause which escalated out of nothing, a war that was more to do with other men's machinations and stupidities in countries far away than with justice. For that, my freedom was denied me and my life almost denied me too. The men who did this, the politicians, *are* stupid, unfeeling, with no understanding of what makes life worth living. Life for me is redeemed by the presence of people like Amy, Mary, Giselle, Anna, and all the unnamed warm and generous women that I have not yet met – it is also made bearable by the generosity, humour and simple humanity of a people such as those who occupy the Aegean, who live sparsely in the worst of conditions, who have nothing and expect less, and yet whose lives are fuller than any person's I have ever known – far fuller than the lives of Alain and his friends, who want for nothing, and yet who have nothing, nothing of true value.

I think of the past month, the various villages I have visited, the simple homes in which I have stayed and been made welcome, the meals I have shared, the kindnesses I have been shown without question by people into whose lives I have wandered for a few days, before I walk on, never to see them again.

I feel that from now on – I have felt it before, but never with such conviction – I must do whatever it is that *I* wish to do with life. The simple fact is that I wish to postpone my future, my decisions, and I wish to continue my stay in this beautiful country until I grow tired of it, whether that happens next year, or never.

If, in order to do this, I need to tell a few small lies to my father, and to call on his money, then so be it. The money is no great moral problem – his cigar allowance alone would buy me three meals a day. The lies? I admit that they bother me slightly, because in the aftermath of the war my parents have been good to me, tolerating a great deal. I am far from being the son for whom they obviously had hopes and expectations. In any case, I may actually be telling my father and mother the truth. Who is to say that I will not return to take up my place at Oxford, next autumn instead of this? I may well decide to apply for a change to classics, and will certainly spend some of my time in Greece visiting those sites I have not yet seen. So it is impossible to say, until then, whether I am lying now or not.

19 July

The letter was not long in coming, and I do not blame my father at all for saying he expects that it will not in any case reach me, that he may as well vainly address it to *poste restante* Timbuctoo as Kavala. I do admit that I have scarcely been noted for reliability during these early months in Greece.

Most important, though, is that it seems he will co-operate, for which I give great hurrahs, and will tonight drink his health in brandy, which I know he will appreciate. His crony at Oxford has told him, over the telephone, that there seems no objection to them postponing the start of my course for twelve months, in view of my war service; although I may have to take a kind of re-admission interview next summer. I shall face that moment when it arrives.

He is rather more circumspect on the subject of money, which comes as absolutely no surprise. He asks me to reassure him concerning the classical sites I have visited, and what I found there that made me wish to stay on! If only I were able to tell him. I stay on with the intention of enjoying myself, and in the hope of discovering others like Anna.

I shall, of course, write in detail to tell him about the points of interest at Delphi, Knossos and elsewhere; though I am forced to remain here in Kavala to await a reply and confirmation that he will remit my allowance at regular intervals to a bank in Athens. I have suggested a figure which I think not too high, as I still have my own pension accruing each month, which can be transferred here if necessary –

and I also promise to repay such advances as father makes whenever I am in a position to do so.

21 July

Kavala itself is a rambling pleasant-enough town, reasonably busy, but I cannot say that it appeals to me in the way that other towns, equally ordinary, somehow manage to appeal. There is a dusty market building here, which buzzes with activity on market days. The wood and canvas stalls groan with goods, and outside on the cracked, dusty pavements, farmers and their noisy wives, who have walked or ridden in from the countryside around, spread out their produce – such colours in the sunlight! A tray of lemons or of oranges assault the eyes with their newness of colour. Sprays of flowers abound, and roughly woven white rugs, and leather-ware in every shade of brown.

The town has a dramatic Roman aqueduct that strides over the houses like some tall pale animal, while the old remains of a Byzantine citadel are said to be hidden, unseen by me, somewhere through a maze of narrow streets that lead upwards behind the harbour.

Whenever I ask my way, it seems that eventually I always find myself walking downwards instead of upwards, returning instead to the harbour. Perhaps it is a local custom to misdirect visitors – or perhaps my Greek is not as good as I imagine it to be!

As there will be no reply from home for several days, I

have decided instead, to buy passage on a ferryboat, to spend the next few days on Thasos, an island only a few miles off the coast.

23 July

This morning the ancient ferry deposited me unceremoniously in Limen, the main town of Thasos. Indeed Thasos does, from first impression live up to its reputation for beauty. Green and hilly, mountainous almost, the slopes are wooded with chestnuts and pines and look delightful. I must explore them while I am here.

At the moment, I am writing this journal in a harbour-front café enjoying the luxury of a cool beer and watching a little of the world of Thasos go by. A dark-skinned, dark-haired woman in blue skirt and jumper, looking rather Turkish in her red headscarf, is beating an octopus remorselessly against the ground, holding it by the tentacles and whacking its body hard against the stone pavement, to tenderise the meat, I presume. I have not yet attempted to eat octopus, although, if it needs to be pummelled like that to render it edible, I am not convinced that the creature is such a delicacy!

The room I have taken is pleasant enough, near the edge of the town, in a small white-washed rooming house located across the road from the house of the family which owns it. It has a garden, with beehives, and is newly built, bright and attractive, which is more than can be said for the family themselves.

A small boy of about seven or eight accosted me as I disembarked from the ferry and asked if I needed a room. An enterprising approach, as I have found in other places. Indicative too, of the increasing numbers of visitors to these islands. This is scarcely surprising, considering the incredible beauty of the country and the modern ease of access. The boy himself was friendly, though on meeting his family it is difficult to see where his good nature sprang from.

They stared at me glumly, as if their faces had been constructed in clay without the ability to smile. The boy's mother, thickset and sullen, showed me the vacant room with hardly a sound! Merely pointing at the low wooden bed, a blue china washbasin and jug, the table and so forth, she indicated the price by writing with her finger against the palm of her hand. It was so cheap, and clean, I decided to take it, despite the sombre nature of its owners, of whom, I imagine, I will not see a great deal in any case.

24 July

Last night I ate in a lively taverna in the main street, and made my attempt at eating an octopus (or at least part of one). I have to say that I feel this is one taste of Greece that I will be making little effort to acquire. Somehow I associate sea creatures with having a rather softer flesh. My only consolation was that it encouraged me to drink great glasses of straw-coloured wine, in an attempt to ease the chewing;

which, in part, conspired to lead me to this morning's little incident.

As I say, I drank last evening a great deal of local wine, for the company was new and very convivial, and although the wine does not affect me now as badly as it might have done a few months ago, it did encourage me to sleep soundly. Even here on the mainland, the weather is so burningly hot at present that I continue to sleep naked. And frequently I also throw back the thin cotton sheet that provides sole cover for the bed in these rooms.

My first recollection of this morning was of a gentle knocking sound. I was in that moment of half-sleep when one wonders if a noise is heard or dreamt. As I was about to drift back into slumber, the door of my room opened slowly and a young Greek girl entered. After a moment spent staring, she muttered a quick apology and went out.

It was only after she had left my room that I became fully awake and aware, not only of my nakedness but also of my state of tumescence. This waking arousal probably happens to most men, certainly it frequently happens to me in the morning, I awake to a feeling of warmth and the fullness of an erection, and of late, with the lack of a female companion, I have taken to pleasuring myself in a drowsy kind of a manner.

It was my own fault. The time was hardly nine o'clock in the morning when the girl's presence woke me, yet I should know well enough by now that this is practically mid-morning by local standards. At least she had sense enough not to scream and throw up her arms in shock at the sight of me – though as a precaution I spent my day well away from my small room in the lodging house, and only came back a few minutes ago, once twilight had fallen over the houses. The owner looks as if he would not take too well to visitors offending his maid.

26 July

I was awake and decently dressed at an early hour both today and yesterday, well before any maid could make an appearance (though I felt sure she would take care not to make the same mistake again). But yesterday she failed to arrive and it was only when I was walking around the almost deserted town and heard the church bells that I realised it was Sunday. One loses track of days when travelling in this manner.

On my walk through the streets I saw my landlord and his wife, who was as sobre-faced as the oldest of matrons in an English church. They greeted me with that almost imperceptible nod of the head which they employ – not so much greeting as grudging acknowledgement. It seems the maid has yet to report what she saw, which is a relief. I had vague nightmares of the local police descending on me and hauling me off to the cells.

Giselle told me a story on one occasion, after we'd spent our day swimming naked in a secluded cove that was backed by steep and barren sides. Naturally, her companions – and I when I was there – took great care not to offend, and only to choose the most inaccessible places to bathe. This was,

Giselle told me with a smile, not due simply to a sense of morality. Apparently the police in this country have their own way of dealing with foreigners who swim naked in Greek waters, which happens a great deal more than one might suppose.

They do not make a fuss, or wait for the swimmers to emerge from the water. Instead, they just remove the clothing and take it to the police station, leaving behind a note stating where the clothes can be reclaimed. Giselle had heard of more than one case where the group involved had no alternative but to walk naked to the police station through the streets of a village to ask for the return of their clothes. Naturally there was also a fine to pay, and the shame.

The villagers had somehow become mysteriously informed of the wrongdoing and were waiting for the miscreants to emerge, so that they could indulge in great laughter at their misfortune and embarrassment. I insisted to Giselle that if that happened to me I would simply wait in hiding until, perhaps, three in the morning, then return to my room, not attempt to reclaim the clothes but collect my things and move swifly on. At which Giselle pronounced that the police would see to it that I could not get into my room.

In all but the largest Greek communities, everyone knows what everyone else is doing and where and how they are living.

Despite all these forewarnings, I walked today for a couple of hours along a track leading away from Limen, and discovered a secluded bay where I was able to swim naked for a short while, being careful to keep my eyes on my clothes and indeed almost the whole rocky coastline. It was such a pleasure to swim, compounding my sense of freedom, that doing so naked was worth the slight risk involved.

I met a strange 'character' as I returned along the track, about twenty minutes walk after leaving the bay. I had sat down on a broken stone wall by the side of the track, and was listening to the eternal buzz of the bees as they flew to or from the many hives that dot the island lanscape. A spoonful of local honey from these bees is like eating scented sunlight, and when mixed with the thick Greek yoghourt it produces a taste that must surely have been the nectar of the Gods.

Ianni Drofolopoulos, I think he said his name was. He shattered my bee-watching peace by crashing through the trees behind me, and stumbling down a bank to the wall where I sat. He carried an old single-barrel shotgun under his arm and resembled an ageing Puck.

At first I was apprehensive, for he rushed at me with such an intent expression on his face. But it seems that he was merely intent on talking. Indeed it was difficult to stop him once he had started, though the conversation might have seemed shorter or more interesting had he been able to speak English, as my own Greek was certainly not up to catching more than the occasional few words. The predominant smell that hung about the man was one of goat; and perhaps it would be better not to try even to identify the others which went into making that brew which he carried about with him. Ianni was bare-footed, wore fairly ordinary if rather gaping black trousers, and above the waist was wrapped in some indefinable garment of goatskin, which could not have smelled stronger when it was still on the goat. In one hand he held the shotgun, in the other he carried what I imagined to be his equivalent of a shepherd's crook; a sturdy piece of wood which he banged on the ground for emphasis in the course of our conversation.

For the most part I simply smiled and nodded, waiting for the torrent to cease so that I might stand and leave, but when he eventually paused in his speech and I made to rise, he put a restraining arm on my shoulder and reached inside his goatskin to produce an unlabelled bottle of red wine, from which he gulped several mouthfuls, spilling a large amount down his unshaven chin. A connoisseur of the grape, evidently! He then handed me the bottle motioning me to drink, and though there was nothing I wanted less in the world than to raise the neck of that bottle to my own lips, I saw no way in which I could refuse this strange and simple man's offer of hospitality.

I pointed out the hives and asked him in my halting Greek what the word for those objects was, and while his attention was diverted I quickly wiped the neck of his bottle before I could bring myself to put it to my lips. As to the wine, it had all the smoothness of molten lava.

Again I tried to leave, and again he placed a restraining hand on me, only this time instead of taking my shoulder to insist I sit down, he gripped my thigh, and gripped it quite firmly. I sat once more, being now not quite sure what to do, and his hand remained on my thigh as he continued to jabber away in a hailstorm of words – a rather apt comparison, now I think about it. A raincoat would have served me well.

It was the hand on my thigh which concerned me most, though. I know full well by now how the Greeks are renowned for their unselfconscious physicality; the friendly arm a man will put round the shoulder of his friend, sometimes even linking arms as they stroll in the street. Yet I also know how the ancients were renowned for something more, and when his goaty fingers crept higher up my thigh I knew the time had come.

I stood and pushed him away, calling him all the swear-words I could muster. I was prepared for him to make trouble, and the glare in his wild eyes made me feel sure he was capable of attacking me. Yet instead of that or of hurling abuse back, he merely trotted up the steep bank and disappeared, just as swiftly and as noisily, crashing away through the trees.

And now that I have recorded that rather odd encounter, I feel fully ready to go in search of a café for my evening meal. Some wine would be good, hopefully pleasanter than the raw firewater served up by that very strange stranger.

27 July

Seagulls wheel above me, swinging in great circles about the stern of this ferry as it ploughs its way through the wine-dark water separating Thasos from the mainland.

Yesterday was indeed a day for strange encounters. Last evening, as I left the door of my lodging house to walk to a café, who should emerge from my landlord's house opposite but the young maid; the first time I had seen her since the incident that other morning.

It was only on seeing her again that I noticed a slight family resemblance – she is undoubtedly the landlord's daughter, though she does not seem to have inherited his dour nature and expression. I must be grateful that they are obviously not aware of the embarrassment I caused her. If, indeed, embarrassment it was? When she saw me and caught my glance she greeted me politely enough, and it was evidently I who was feeling the more awkward about what had happened.

I returned her greeting hesitantly and said, in Greek, what a beautiful evening it was. She replied in halting English, saying that, yes, it was a beautiful evening, adding that she was learning English but did not have much opportunity to speak it – only when English visitors came to stay. I immediately offered to talk English to her, and invited her to dine with me. Of course, I knew as soon as I said it that this would not be possible. A young Greek girl could no more dine alone with a single and foreign man, than walk naked through the streets. But I had made the remark as I would to any other woman. She confirmed that she could not possibly dine with me but thanked me sincerely enough for the invitation, then said that we must not talk too long in the street. I suggested that we could walk together to wherever she was going, but the girl said that it would not be right and hurried off in front of me.

As I ate my meal at a quiet café, I reflected upon the very different attitudes that exist in Greece and in England. Strange that there are so many aspects of the Greek way of life whose freedom I have praised – the open and friendly nature of the people, the comparative lack for foreigners of that awful rigid structure that petrifies our own society, certainly the lack of formality and nonsensical politeness that permeates England. And yet the young women in England, hemmed in as they are, are free as birds compared to the young women in Greece. I could not even exchange a few words in the street without a girl becoming concerned that we should be seen and no doubt her 'loose' behaviour commented upon.

Her young brother can run free in the streets, yet her way of life is still mediaeval compared with that of a young English girl, and is positively still in the Stone Age when one thinks of Giselle.

The ferry is about to pull into Kavala, where I have come to see if there is any mail from England. My thoughts last night only confirmed to me how right I am to stay travelling. How can I judge my own way of life until I have seen how other people live and make their decisions? At home the talk was all of 'After you go to university, you must take up your career'; and one can be swept along with this – better by far to see other people making other choices, and realise there are always a hundred, if not a thousand, alternative futures.

28 July

I have returned to Thasos, bringing with me a letter from

father in which he confirms that he will grant me an allowance of £10 per month for the next twelve months. This, together with my pension, half of which he has remitted, will be more than enough to enable me to continue to live and travel adequately. Thank you, father! In typical fashion, he slightly soured his gesture by announcing that I can repay him once I have got this travelling nonsense out of my head. It seems there has also been a letter of confirmation from Oxford, as to my delaying my arrival by twelve months, subject to satisfactory re-interview should I change subjects in the meantime.

I was able to exchange a few words with the young maid this morning. She was tidying my room when I returned from breakfast in a café to collect such things as I would need for a walk, which is turning out to be glorious, high into the scrub-covered hills with beautiful, breathtaking views across to the slightly misty mainland. Not so beautiful was the thick-bodied snake I almost trod on as I made my way up a short-cut through woods!

I asked the maid, Catarina, whether I could help her with her English. Catarina immediately said that she would appreciate it if I could, but added after a moment's silence that it would be difficult because of her parents. We should not be seen together or neighbours' tongues would start wagging. I feel sure there is something troubling this girl, something more than mere propriety. I said that I would be glad to help if there was a way we could meet without causing many problems for her. She thanked me, smiled slightly and left the room.

29 July

This morning I deliberately waited a while before leaving for breakfast, in the hope of talking more with Catarina – she seems gentle and quiet, yet troubled and somehow trapped, as if prevented from even talking by the custom of her country.

When she came in – knocking loudly several times – we talked in English as she worked. I asked innocently if she was ever allowed a day off, so that we might have time to talk a little. I have been the only visitor present in this guesthouse since my arrival, so it cannot require too much work of her.

Catarina said, rather nervously, that tomorrow her parents were to make one of their monthly trips to the market at Kavala, but that she was not allowed to go with them.

We could talk, she said, but must not be seen speaking together, as this would be sure to get back to her father and mother. They were both very strict about her behaviour. Stricter by far than the parents of her friends, which must mean very bad indeed.

I immediately described to her the beach I had found a few days ago, where we could talk in complete privacy. She could bring any English books she had, and we could meet somewhere along the track. Catarina considered this in silence for a time, temptation wrestling with uncertainty, then said doubtfully that it was unusual for a young woman to walk alone, but not so remarkable as to get her into trouble should anyone see her. And so she agreed.

I told her again where to walk and promised her I would

sit by the road and wait for her at a point where a small path branches off the winding track and goes down to the sea, then no-one would see us together. I suggested that she might like a swim, but she declined, saying that she never swam and had no costume. I thought better of saying one did not need a costume. She seemed so hesitant about the whole matter that I would not want to frighten her away.

I feel curious – and perhaps doubtful – about my own motives in all this. Catarina is undoubtedly an attractive girl. Her figure is slim and her skin olive-coloured and smooth. If it were not for her circumstances, I should certainly want to bed her if this were possible. But I also want simply to talk to her – to discover what wealth of emotion needs be hidden by such a quiet exterior, not only for her but for all the other young women who live such sheltered existences here. For the most part, I imagine, they accept what life offers, but what thoughts I wonder do simmer behind those lovely olive faces, with their dark and downcast eyes?

1 August

This episode I shall have to write out in full, but with a warm – and pray peaceful – Sunday afternoon in prospect, and myself with nothing more to do than sit quietly in the shade and let my confusion subside, that shall be no hardship.

We had arranged to meet at about noon, when Catarina

would have had a chance to finish her work and prepare part of the supper for her parents' return in the evening. She would need to be back by late afternoon, she had said. In fact I set off mid-morning, with the hope of having a swim before she arrived – a swim much welcomed after an hour's walk in this heat, even though the track is often sheltered by groves, when not lined by the rows of bee-hives. Their intense, almost angry buzz, like the chirruping of the cicadas, seems a sound that should only be heard on the hottest days.

I swam naked in complete seclusion, my only companions being the small black fish that slithered in the warm sea around me. It was interesting to watch them to see how they reacted to this invader of their water. Some swam up and almost rubbed against my legs, while the occasional one would dart in to see if I was in any way edible, causing no more than a slight sucking feeling for the tiniest fraction of a second. I saw no people, only the occasional fishing boat in the distance sailing into or out of Limen, so far away and so tiny that the craft could have been unmanned.

I dried and dressed long before Catarina arrived, and sat up by the track listening to the summer sounds around me, watching the sparrows fighting and flitting in the trees. No-one else appeared, so I shut my eyes and enjoyed the welcome peace and tranquility: though I have come to expect this as a regular part of Greek landscape and life.

I heard Catarina before I saw her, and waved as she emerged through olive trees round the bend in the track. I led the way down to the beach, where we sat in silent harmony for a time as she soaked up the scene.

The conversation was slow in coming. She had brought her books, but when I suggested we read from them she said she would prefer simply to try to talk to me in English, as she thought this would be the best way to learn – her grasp of the language is remarkably good, it is her confidence which is lacking.

She has a wide vocabulary, though some of her words I could not understand because of the strange pronunciation – this she lacks practice in. I asked why she wanted to learn the language. At first she said it was because of the visitors who were starting to come to the island. Indeed, there were several visitors in the town this week, though her young brother had not managed to work his charm on them at the harbour as he had done on me.

After talking of other things, she returned hesitantly to the subject and asked if she could reveal a secret. I said she could. Whereupon she confided that the real reason she wished to learn was so that she could leave Thasos. She wanted to go to America. Taki, an uncle of hers, went there before the war and now owned three restaurants in Chicago. In a letter to her parents, he had suggested that Catarina come to work for him, good Greek girls were hard to find, but her mother and father were outraged at the idea.

To them, the place of a good Greek girl was at home. Her father used to beat her when she was a child, and still hit her brother, and though he had stopped when she grew older, she had never forgotten it, nor forgiven him. She had wanted to escape ever since – escape so far that there was no chance of anyone following to force her to return.

Since then she had worked away in silence on her

ambition, learning English and saving what little money she could towards the cost of the cheapest sea crossing she could find. She still had some way to go, but one day she would walk out, and go to Athens to get the papers. The first her family would know of where she was would be when they received a letter from Chicago. This name evidently held some kind of mythical charm, and she pronounced it quite enchantingly as Zhicag*o*, with an accent on the last letter.

Her purpose in admitting all this was to enable her to question me about the country. What did I know of America? she asked. Was it as big as her uncle described it? I said, I thought so. She was so determined to go that it would not have mattered what I said. She was simply thirsty for any information about the place, and anything bad I might have said would have been discounted. Not that I did say anything bad, for I could see the fierce keenness in her dark eyes, and encouraged her in her dream. I did not want to imagine her as an old woman, still living in the same town, still cleaning out rooms for summer visitors, regretting the chances she had missed when young. And I thought of my own situation, of what I had discovered about myself and about others in my travels.

In her enthusiasm to tell me about her dreams and plans, Catarina laid her hand gently on my arm, a most unusually forthright gesture for a Greek girl; but when she stopped talking she gazed firmly at me and left it there, knowing full well how forward she was being. She then said quietly that in America, too, perhaps she would meet a husband. Adding, open-eyed, that she had never lain with a man. More than that, the morning she had come into my room was the first time she had ever seen a naked man.

I asked her with a smile if she was shocked, but she said that she was not. She had been a little embarrassed but more curious than anything, and would have looked for longer had I been asleep! I took her hand and if my feelings had been mixed before, they were now tumbling over themselves.

I had not made love for several weeks, despite that in my time in Greece I had developed quite an appetite for the act. I was sure that she wished me to take her, if only for her own powerful curiosity, for she was strong-willed for all her outward sweetness. I could feel the first stirrings in me. There could surely be no better setting for love-making than that deserted sun-filled beach, but I also knew that if we did we would be taking a great risk, for I had certainly not gone prepared. Did she even know the risks? All of these thoughts jostled for attention in my head but I could hardly discuss them with Catarina.

Instead, I decided to let nature take what course it would. I lifted her fingers to my lips and kissed them gently, then leaned across and kissed her own full lips, which were unpractised but more than welcoming. We lay back on a rock amid the sand and embraced. By now I was being driven by my desire and I began slowly to unbutton the front of her simple dress, revealing her full breasts which felt warm and firm beneath my kisses. I ran my tongue around one of her dark nipples and felt it rise. Her hand found my hardness and she said quietly that she wanted to see me again, and pushed at the waistband of my trousers, too hurried to consider undoing the belt buckle, which I did for her. Catarina pushed my trousers down around my thighs, then smiled as she saw my penis again, gorged to its full hardness. Her fingers caressed it tentatively, her eyes fixed on its tip, then she gripped the shaft firmly, closing her eyes as she did so, and though she had told me she had never lain with a man, I could sense in that moment that she knew what it was like to have a man inside her and filling her.

She caressed me again and asked me in her plain English to do 'it' to her, to show her what a man did when he lay with a woman. I said fiercely that I could not, it was necessary to wear something to prevent her from becoming pregnant. At which she told me that she had heard that, but nevertheless was prepared to lie with me, though I said again that I could not.

'I will probably be going away soon,' I told her, and if she found that she was pregnant what would happen to her in a town like this? She shrugged, as if she did not know, but I was sure that she did and the truth was so shocking that she was keeping it from me.

'What of your dream?' I asked. With a baby to take care of, she might never achieve her ambition of going to America, of working there and seeing all that there was to see. To which Catarina said that perhaps, with a baby, they would *send* her to America, and I wondered briefly if this indeed was her purpose.

She too was juggling with ideas and new feelings that she did not understand, all for this driving physical passion that it is so difficult to resist.

Catarina continued to squeeze my shaft and implored me to put myself into her, just for a short time and 'not to make a baby' as she described it, which was a fairly primitive description of *coitus interruptus.* Feeling this could do no harm, as long as I continued to control myself, I pushed her white dress up around her waist, revealing, to my surprise, not the baggy all-covering white drawers I had somehow expected, but a briefer pair of pink pants that stretched over her mound and might have come from Giselle's wardrobe. She asked me if I liked them, and said that she had bought them a year ago on her only visit to Athens, her special 'pantaloni' she called them, which she had bought for America and wore when she wanted to feel and look modern.

This she most certainly did, I kissed her bare breasts and I rubbed my hand across her soft stomach, pushing my fingers below the waistband of her pants, to feel the first few curly hairs tangle round my fingertips. I pulled down the front a little to reveal those black curls, and moved my hand down between her trembling legs.

It was then – fate willing – that I felt the most incredible sting in my buttocks, as if I had been stabbed by a hot needle, and I yelled and turned to see myself pierced by one of the island's enormous bees! I brushed the insect away, foolishly breaking the sting and the insect shuddered across the sand, giving out a ceaseless angry buzzing. Catarina began to giggle as I struggled to my knees, much impeded by my trousers, and endeavoured to examine my rear to see what might be done about the sting, the pain from which had not diminished in the least. No doubt I did present a comical sight, as my shaft was still hard and bobbing about, poking out from under the front of my shirt, but I was enraged at Catarina's giggles – she had returned her skirt to more decorous lengths and was buttoning up the front.

I tried in vain to squeeze out the sting but was anxious that it should not break off.

'Pull out the sting,' I yelled at her, 'and for God's sake, stop laughing, I'm in agony.' She controlled her giggles enough to sit up, although the sight of my shaft now visibly shrinking almost set her off again.

I lay face down on the sand feeling extremely undignified, while Catarina began to squeeze out the sting. It took a great deal of manipulation, and her long fingernails against my flesh made me wonder which was the worse agony, but eventually the sting emerged to her satisfaction. She told me to wait there, and she walked away from the beach, following the winding trail up towards the main track. Not that I could do very much else, lying face down with my trousers around my knees and my rear burning from the combination of bee-sting and hot sun. But I was not, as I thought, deserted.

After a few moments, Catarina emerged again from the greenery at the top of the slope, carrying a leaf, the size of a large dock, but a darker green and even more leathery. This she placed in her mouth and chewed, as she knelt beside me. The mush produced was placed over the sting as a kind of poultice. Demanding my handkerchief, Caterina took it and tied it to her own as if knotting together two sheets. The sting was then bandaged, the material winding between my legs and up around my hip.

It hardly needs noting that all thoughts of passion had, by this time, long disappeared; which was perhaps just as well, given the circumstances. I restored some dignity by hitching up my trousers, and gave Catarina a good thirty minutes to make her way home ahead of me.

This particular episode is long in the telling, but I needs must recount the details while fresh in my mind – for it was not yet over by any means! The ache in my wrist and fingers means that the recording must be over for a moment. A mid-afternoon glass of ouzo will, however, no doubt revive my strength.

My strength maybe, but quite what the ouzo might do for my writing ability I will discover. The effect of drink in this heat is enervating, yet what a delight is the taste of that sharp cold aniseed – like the island sounds I have already described, it seems that this drink was made to be drunk in the sun.

Despite a renewed vow that I would not endeavour to take advantage of Catarina, I thought repeatedly of her that night; recalling in detail the glimpses I had been given of her dark body, and my member was hard with its need of a woman. This forced abstinence is not easy to endure!

I exchanged brief words with her yesterday morning as she cleaned my room, and there was a certain lightness between us, as if she was always on the verge of laughing at the previous day's events, but also, I think, because she felt relief that she had shared her secret with someone. I did wonder quite what would happen next; whether we might steal time together should her parents again be away: although her father is out tending his olive fields and orchards daily, her mother seems never more than a few yards from the house morning till night, day after day.

In the late morning, I was seated in one of my favourite cafés in Limen, writing correspondence to friends at home. Suddenly I was startled to see Catarina, evidently distressed, hurrying along the crowded street towards me. One of her eyes was badly swollen and there were other severe bruises on her face and bare arms. She told me urgently to leave at once, that her father had returned early from the fields and had immediately set about beating her, yelling that she was a slut and a whore, and had been seen to be indecent with the Englishman.

I asked, somewhat bewilderedly, how he had found out about us. 'Some half-crazed goatman,' she said, 'had watched us.'

I knew at once. It had to be that wretched creature who had accosted me earlier; for it was along that road that I had encountered him. Catarina had denied the story, insisting that the man was crazed and a notorious liar. But her father took him at his word, having apparently suspected me for some days.

All this urgent conversation took place in the main street, in Catarina's halting English, much to the frustration of half the street, who were staring at us in undisguised curiosity. Catarina's words were punctuated by her continued insistence that I should leave. I said, of course, that I would not go, that I would never allow anyone to hit her in that way. At which she smiled sadly. I simply did not understand, she told me. After beating her, her father went to fetch his gun, and she had run from the house to find me and warn me, knowing my favourite places.

Although Catarina had managed to flee from her father by running down side streets before cutting into the main street, it could not be long before he found me. And when he did so, she assured me, he would have no hesitation in shooting me down there in the street, in full view of all, knowing that no witnesses would see who had killed the Englishman – not when they knew the cause.

At last I recognised the true panic in her eyes; realised that I must act immediately. Yet how could I leave her to a bully of a father? Catarina told me not to worry, she was still a virgin, he would do no worse than the beating she had been given already. As for her future, she would be on the ferry for Kavala and away on a train to Athens before her parents even knew where she was. There she would find a job and earn the rest of the money she needed for her ticket to America.

I told her quickly where I had been staying in Kavala, then fled along the street, away from the direction of her house. I did not at first know where I was going, but I listed mentally the possessions I had with me and was relieved to discover that I did at least have everything vital.

I slowed to a walk, shunning the harbour and grateful for the anonymity of the backstreets. I recall thinking that this couldn't really be happening. It was as if I was trapped in a dream. It brought home, too, how easy it was to offend custom and traditions. I had made every attempt to be circumspect, discreet, careful not to offend the morality of a country whose people had become dear to me, yet whose way of life was very different in these respects to my own awakening ideas.

As I gathered my thoughts I realised that unconsciously I was heading in the direction of Ormos Prinou, a village to which I had walked one day. This, to my blessed relief, was where the Kavala ferry called before it reached Limen. The distance overland from Limen to Ormos Prinou was a good and rugged ten miles, yet I could hardly double back and sit by the harbour in Limen while waiting for the ferry. It was then I suddenly realised the tiny dimensions of the island!

It sounds dramatic to say that I felt trapped, yet it was true. I needed to reach the ferry. Without a ferry to take me away, and with the intricate network of Catarina's friends and relatives, where within the island could I flee to escape her father?

I trekked along the narrow road as briskly as I could: as fit as I consider myself to be even with my wretched leg, the prospect of a ten-mile run in the blistering mid-day heat was not realistic. And at every sound of mule-clop or footstep, I leapt into the nearest ditch or behind the first tree, imagining some kind of armed gang hunting me down without mercy. Fortunately I saw nothing more threatening than an old couple heading for Limen, the woman perched precariously on top of the mule, atop two sacks of water-melons.

It was late afternoon and growing cooler when I reached Ormos Prinou; my mouth was so dry it felt as though it were filled with ashes. I sat in the village's one café and gulped down several tumblers of water – first being sure to take an inconspicuous seat, from where I could make a hasty exit if necessary.

In a state of extreme anxiety I waited for the last ferry to arrive – after Prinou it would call at Limen before it returned to Kavala. But there seemed to me to be no alternative to taking this boat. I boarded apprehensively and as the vessel approached Limen I buried myself on the far side of the deck away from the crowd gathered on the quay, hoping I would hear the disturbance if a man with a shotgun tried to get on board to search the decks.

Quite what I would have done I am not sure – jump overboard and swim in a straight line away from the boat, or possibly a straight line downwards!

Fortunately, I did not need to do anything. I have no idea whether Catarina's father was on that harbour front or not. If he was he presumably thought that I would attempt to board the ferry there, for nothing untoward happened and I breathed a sigh of great relief when I felt the ferry move at last and we parted the waves towards Kavala.

3 August

What a marathon account! But what a tale. As I had hoped, Catarina did arrive at the hotel I'd described, and I greeted her warmly, still partly shocked to see that a man could black the eye of a girl; yet I, more than most, should know about the brutalities of which man is capable.

She assured me that nothing further had happened to her that evening, except for being bullied and shoved, and continually told what disgrace she had brought to the family.

Catarina also said her father, the goatherd and her cousins had hunted high and low through Limen for me; but as there were several exits from the town and they knew I had received advance warning of the pursuit, they eventually gave up the chase: though her father did wait by the harbour to attend to every ferry that left that afternoon, his gun cocked.

Catarina had made good her escape, hiding her few belongings in an out-house, then retrieving them upon the pretext of visiting the shops. This she timed with the arrival of the ferry, sneaked on board and, like me, was away.

We had little time to spend together, and that innocent, as she did not wish to stay long in Kavala, but naturally wished to reach Athens as soon as was possible. How strange that with no love lost between them, her family should still want to tie her to the home. Except, I suppose, that she was capable of working.

I admire Catarina, and I wish her well. She did not know where she would be staying in Athens, and somehow I feel it is right that we should not attempt to keep in touch with each other. We seem to have brought an alarming amount of trouble upon ourselves during our brief liaison.

I offered Catarina a small amount of money towards her trip to America – I am sure she will make it, and dearly wish that she prospers and is happy there – but she refused, as I expected. I do not have a great deal as, of course, I have had to replace much of my clothing and the bag that I lost at her father's house, but I took slightly more than I could spare and rolled the notes tightly into a bundle. I surreptitiously pushed this deep into her bag, as I carried it to the bus station for her. By the time she discovers the money she will have no means of returning it. I feel responsible for what has happened to that poor girl. Also, the money means much less to me that it does to her. Even if it merely enables her to reach America one week sooner, then it will be worth it. More funds are now on their way here from my bank in Athens, or so I hope!

10 August

I feel as if I am a fugitive on the run, or one of those poor wretches who could take no more of the trenches and hoped to find freedom in the French countryside – many of them only succeeding in finding their freedom in the bullet of a firing squad.

My money arrived last week from Athens, for which I am profoundly grateful. A short time after collecting the money, I was seated on a wooden bench, in the welcoming shade of a few small trees, considering my next course of direction, when necessity made the choice for me. I saw – though he did not see me – the frighteningly familiar figure of Caterina's father approaching slowly down the street. I spotted him through the trees. Fortunately, he had not looked my way but his purposeful stride left me in no doubt of his intent, even if he was not quite so obviously armed as he might have dared in Limen. I pitied him briefly, and think he thought Catarina and I would be together as he searched through Kavala's labyrinthine streets.

Before he could look my way I was gone, back to my hotel. Packing my rather strange collection of clothes in a new leather bag took seconds rather than minutes, then I slipped out and headed for the station, to take the first bus in whatever direction.

This explains my presence in Thessaloniki, where I now kick my heels still uncertain where next to travel. My inclination to allow chance to be my guide has been somewhat upset, given what serendipity has led me to!

12 August

I had a haunting conversation this afternoon with an American who runs a charming café here, where I had gone for a mid-afternoon bowl of yoghourt and honey.

The café looked inviting with its handful of tables and chairs set out beneath the trees in a small park opposite. I assumed the woman who came to attend to me was Greek. She wore her widow's weeds and addressed me in Greek, but after I had ordered she asked eagerly if I was American – and was only slightly disappointed to discover that I was merely English. I think she had hoped I would be from her home state, and ideally her home town – though quite where her home town was, was evidently causing her a great deal of bother.

She was not too busy, and when she returned with my yoghourt and honey she sat beside me and talked. It seemed there were not many English-speaking visitors in Thessaloniki, it having little to offer by way of sea or ruins.

Those that do visit the city seldom venture to her quarter, which is a little out of the way but the kind of area I like to find in my wanderings.

How sad she was feeling, and isolated, even among her Greek family. I supposed her to be about forty years of age, perhaps less – in the town of Tucson where she grew up, she had been a waitress in a Greek restaurant. An emigrant from Thessaloniki had arrived as a waiter, and soon became assistant manager. They were married within months, and after a few years of hard saving, and of talk about the beauty of his native Greece, they had come to live here, making the down payment on the café with their savings.

Her husband had not been young and she herself had been in her thirties when they married. They had not been running the café for long when he died of heart failure.

Now she was trying to sell up but without luck. She wanted to return to Tucson, and needs must sell the business in order to raise her fare home. Her husband's family has been kind to her, but she is still a stranger and wants very much to be home again; despite having no family now to return to in Tucson. She also talks of trying to start again, in New York or elsewhere. But her eyes lack fire and I sensed her looking at me as if I were able to tell her what she should do, where she should go.

I wished her luck, and said that I will call in to the café again, yet I know already that I will not.

19 August

I arrived this evening at Nauplia, and how happy I am to be here! The bus journey from Athens was a nightmare. The temperature inside the ancient bus was so high that much of the produce being carried by its passengers must have arrived cooked. I arrived roasted, of that I am sure; and gasping for air and a little space.

By the time we arrived and I stepped down from the bus, it felt strange not to have a bony elbow in my face, so accustomed had I become to that discomfort, not to mention the occasional intrusion of more intimate parts of people's anatomies as they squeezed past me in my seat.

I arrived late and so took the first room I inspected. It is small and having but a small window is no doubt also dark during the day. Nauplia, however, seems worth any inconvenience, being much more the kind of place that I like. Even on my brief evening's acquaintance, it looks perhaps the most beautiful town I have yet seen.

The old buildings cling precariously to the sides of a small rocky promontory guarding a harbour. The houses are ancient, peeling and delightful, with small balconies that jut out above one's head, and which are frequently festooned with multi-coloured washing drying in the sun. At the very top of the promontory is the citadel, guarding over the town like a benevolent aristocrat, ever-ready to protect the inhabitants but otherwise content to bask elegantly in the sun looking handsome.

I have come here to make my long-promised visit to the theatre at Epidavros – pledged to myself as well as to Anna, all those months ago. Anna did say that I must visit the site while here in Greece, and, though I know I have all the time in the world in which to make this visit, I want to do so before the summer is out.

Nauplia is especially welcoming after Thessalonika and a few days in Athens, spent collecting mail and money, and finding out how best to see Epidavros. The cities are become less attractive to me, despite a certain fascination and an increased chance of female company. My 'near-experience' with Catarina makes me long for intimacy . . . I still ache as I remember my fingers touching her stomach, and tangling the hairs that began just below.

20 August

The café in which I sit is quiet and friendly. The coffee is excellent, and a rough canvas awning provides shade from the outrageous mid-day sun.

Nauplia is the kind of town in which there is little to see, yet how good it is to be here. When I write there is little to see, I mean in the sense of a city where I feel I must inspect the museums, visit famous streets, gaze on old statues, and see crumbling and even more famous ruins.

In Nauplia I feel happy to wander the winding streets, sit in cheap cafés writing and reading, perhaps I would even be content to live here for a time. I may even do that!

I have started to have thoughts, though, of spending the coming autumn visiting the islands, with the exception of Thasos and anything within a hundred miles of the place! Or perhaps passing the winter in Crete. The Great Island would seem to have the advantage, not only of being the southernmost part of Greece and therefore, I hope, slightly milder in the depths of December, but also of being large enough to satisfy my restless nature.

The buses travel to Epidavros from here every day, only a short journey, but unless I am to rush there this afternoon I think I will leave my visit until Monday. Saturday and Sunday are sure to bring an influx of visitors, and I much prefer to see special places when they are quiet.

It seems somehow more in keeping with the spirit of these sites, yet I am sure that historically it is false. In their prime, such places must have been every bit as busy and bustling as when now filled with visitors. Yet I still prefer to see them under more tranquil conditions.

22 August

Sunday afternoon. I have chosen a welcome seat in the shade of a pleasant yet simple hotel. I moved in last night from the small dingy room I had taken in a side-street. My new room looks out into the harbour, where fishing boats come and go like restless birds back and forth to their nest.

Last night I was a predator on the prowl. There are foreign visitors in this town, but no women alone that I could see. I shamelessly reconnoitred the streets with the express purpose of seeking out a woman and making contact. Instead of choosing my restaurant for supper by looking at the menu or the price I looked at the customers. I was out of luck, however, as all those who were evidently foreign were also in couples.

I eventually dined well (and cheaply) in a large open restaurant, where a large foreign group were eating at several tables pushed together. I studied them as I slowly ate my steak of grilled swordfish, trying to see if any of the various attractive young women were unattached, but from the friendliness and intimate glances being exchanged, I think not. At least I attempted to seek out some company, even if in a rather unashamed manner.

I have been thinking again about the winter. I contemplate finding somewhere quiet yet delightful like Nauplia, or Hania in Crete, and spending some time trying to write. I do re-read and revise these diaries, and am happy to have a record – even if incomplete – of so much that has happened to me. Yet I wonder, too, if I might not shape them into something more. A work of fiction, perhaps, or even a more formal book of travel writing – though some sections that are of interest to me would certainly have to be removed!

But these are mere thoughts. I no longer have the fear that I absolutely cannot write, though I do know I will never be a great and a moving writer. Part of my uncertainty is that I have been trying to emulate the people I admire. To me, the beauty of a poem is the finest achievement, yet this is simply not the kind of thing I can write well.

When I met Sassoon and Graves in France, both already fine poets, I wanted to be them, and produce the kind of work they write, because I was seeking their approval. Yet I can never ever hope to be on the same level. I do believe, though, that I am just coming to understand more human actions; sometimes even see through the skin to glimpse the soul beneath. In the same way, also, one sees through the skin of the earth to its soul beneath; the spirit that moves in a place like Nauplia or a valley like Delphi, or a sea like the Aegean.

23 August

A special heart beats at Epidavros, of that I am certain. Set in a hot and arid plain of harsh fields, trees and flowers, a land occupied by skinny sheep and goats, one approaches the ancient theatre obliquely, suddenly coming upon the stage then seeing the rising banks of stone seats sweeping round in an arena. The effect is magnificent. A feeling of unrestrained awe pervades, of hushed silence; as if a performance were always about to begin. What a sight it would be to behold a performance of one of the great classical dramatists in that setting.

Climbing the slope to the highest circle of seats, I could hear people below calling to their friends, testing the theatre's famed acoustics. Indeed I could hear every syllable, ringing out in the clear summer air, like the note of a fingernail tapped against fine crystal. It is hard, too, to imagine a more fitting backdrop than that sweep of smoke-grey countryside behind the stage, which leads up to the mountains beyond. I sat there on a stone bench and felt time slip away as I imagined the sun going down, golden rays sweeping across the immortals' sky like a shimmer of burning sheets. As does the Acropolis, this theatre holds a special magic within its harsh stone; a faint echo of every person who has passed through and a hint of the lives of those to come.

It was with great reluctance that I descended the steps between a bank of stone seats, noting the crumbling ends of the structure where stone fell away as if the building merged quite naturally into the earth. I walked down a meandering path to where uncovered slabs and stones marked other lesser buildings, being freed from the earth to breathe again the pure Greek air.

Young students were working the site and uneasy memories came tumbling back, of days in Delphi, so recent and yet so distant. A battered wooden sign announced that the work was being co-ordinated by the Greek Archaeological Society, yet many of the faces there were fair, with hair blond ... and blonde. Foreign archaeology students like Anna, no doubt, or perhaps classics students here just for the summer, working for a few drachmae and their board and lodging.

My eyes took in all this and more; more than just the general view of an ancient site and workers digging, fetching and carrying. I was looking for specific views too, of female students; seeking that exchange of looks which, though perhaps brief, can say so much. The moment came and with it the look, from a blonde girl who had detached herself from a working party and approached me along a path, carrying carefully a small box in which, no doubt, some fragile object was placed. The look said merely that she had noticed me, though I could not have said whether she held a wish that I should speak to her or not. That she was aware of me, I was left in no doubt by the flicker of pale eyes towards me, then away again.

As the blonde girl approached I smiled and addressed her in English – in the hope that she would understand – asking politely what she had found. Holding the wooden box in her slender fingers, she lowered it to show me a glittering fragment.

'Part of a pot,' she told me, 'or perhaps the decorated back of a comb. It is hard exactly to say until it is examined.'

I asked the girl a few more questions, once it became evident that she did not object to talking for a while.

But then I asked her where she came from. 'Germany,' she replied.

I cannot explain the feeling that overcame me, but it was as if my thoughts had been muffled by wool. I could neither think clearly nor respond, and whatever words I spoke were simply mouthed nonsense, sounds that someone else was putting into my mouth.

This girl was the first German I had met since the war – not that I met many alive then. Despite the fact that she was attractive, my behaviour was governed by some stronger instinct. I cannot recall what I said but I tried to smile politely as I explained hurriedly that I had to move on.

The encounter has quite shaken me. I thought that by writing first of the theatre I might more calmly describe the sequel, but even now the confused emotions come rushing back to engulf me. Yet the girl seemed not to have responded in the same violent manner, and she must surely have realised I was English.

If I react in this way to a young girl, how on earth will I behave if I ever meet a German man? Perhaps even meet one of my age, one who was lined up against me in the trenches.

Who is to say that there is not some German equivalent of me even now travelling about in Greece, seeking that peace and the pleasure that have so far eluded him?

25 August

In trying to unravel my feelings, I tell myself that I have behaved in a stupid manner. Surely, I harbour no hatred for individual Germans, any more than I would like them to hold any hatred for me? I who so despised the false hysteria of feeling between our two countries.

Yet it was a German rifle, its trigger pulled by a German soldier, which fired the bullet that so nearly ended my own life. No matter what the intellect says, the heart and soul cannot just forget such a thing.

What must that girl think? For although I was not directly impolite, she could not have failed to notice what my reaction was to her simple statement that she was German. Even if my sudden departure came some sentences afterwards, the cause must have been evident. Shameful that after all these months in Greece, when I have been shown such kindness and extolled it in others, in letters home and in these pages, that I have not learned sufficiently by their example to behave with civility and compassion when I am eventually tested. How easy it is to be friendly to one's friends – that is no sign of warmth in one's heart, the real test is how one reacts to a declared enemy.

26 August

It seems I have been given a chance to redeem myself. This morning, while hunting in a dusty old shop in the backstreets of Nauplia for a new diary and some envelopes, I saw the fair-haired German girl. I put down my intended purchases and hurried on swiftly as I could after her. The shop owner called to me to enquire if she was a friend of mine, and I think I replied 'I hope', in any case he laughed as I went through the door.

As I caught up with her, I said 'Hello,' and the girl stopped to look at me, then greeted me with a slight smile which seemed genuine. I said it was good to see her again and attempted to explain, rather awkwardly, that I was sorry I had rushed away the other day. She said, honestly, that she had not noticed, and then accepted my hurried offer to buy her coffee. Her name, I learned, was Lina.

As we sat in a café by the harbour and chatted, I was talking about one thing while thinking about something else. If Lina had genuinely not noticed, then why should I explain it and risk embarrassing her? It was up to me to sort out my own feelings, yet in order to help myself I must talk to someone. I have thought before that when thoughts are jumbled like a tangle of string, one hopes that someone else will find the end and draw it out, wrapping the string into a ball, making order out of the chaos.

I asked her hesitantly if she would like to dine with me one evening, and we have agreed on tomorrow. Tonight Lina has to attend a talk about progress on the archaeological site. We parted after our cup of coffee because she had to make some purchases for the site office before catching the next bus back. She is, as I suspected, another archaeology student, here in Greece only for the summer – which is now almost over.

28 August

Last night, during the meal, I was perhaps over-anxious to clear the air between us, and very quickly introduced my reaction to her when we first met. I talked at great length of my experiences, explaining about my years in the army, most of them in direct combat with German troops. I did not mention my own wound, but talked of friends I had lost, of awful injuries I had seen, and told her how I had reacted with hostility when I heard her say she was German. I told her also that she was the first German person I had met since the war.

I think I tried too hard to justify myself, for Lina simply said, 'I am sorry that you feel this way. My brother and father were killed in the war, but I do not blame you for this.'

We were silent for a time, then I said truthfully that I was sorry about the losses she and her family had suffered; that of course I did not blame her for the things I had seen, yet the whole episode had been so intense and confusing that the very word *German* had resonances it might never lose. I tried to explain too my own feelings about the futility, the horror of war and the needless waste of the lives of a whole generation, and by the time I was finished I realised that I had gripped her hand as I stared fiercely into her eyes. I smiled and let go her hand and noticed the white skin across the knuckles where I had squeezed it.

At that point, our first course arrived, a plate of the pink cod's roe I love so much. Thankfully, this broke the rather intense mood. Thereafter, we both relaxed and talked about our travels in Greece, and about Berlin, her home city, and her ambitions to become a doctor of archaeology.

It was Lina who returned first to the subject, asking about conditions in the trenches, curious to have first-hand information, for it seems, as with our army, little has been forthcoming from the authorities.

The bus is now here.

It is difficult to write, the ride from Nauplia is so bumpy it feels as if the bus must have square wheels. I am on my way to Epidavros to see Lina (they work even on Saturdays) and to sit in the theatre once more.

This is like Delphi again and visiting Anna. Perhaps life goes in almost connecting spirals instead of a straight line. It certainly seems so – I think I have left something behind, only to pass it again, seeing it from a different angle.

More later, this is impossible.

The great theatre is busy then quiet, quiet then busy. A crowded bus will suddenly arrive, unload and a wave of people will wash in, like waves into a rock pool, filling every corner, exploring, slapping with noise, and will then retreat again; the place is left as if untouched, except for the two or three people like myself, seemingly content to stay here a while.

I notice how spread out we stragglers are – far to my right, about half-way down the rows of stone seats, an elderly European couple sit and gaze, exchanging the occasional word or pointing to something of interest in the landscape. To my left, perhaps forty or fifty yards away, a solitary and bearded young man sits, in dark blue shirt and trousers, with a large straw hat. He looks like an artist but does not sketch, merely looks around him and smokes a cigarette. Then another wave of visitors rolls in, up and over the seating to the back – calling – down again to inspect the stage, and out. Sometimes they leave a straggler to join us, as if stranded on the rocks. Another wave, and already the elderly couple have been swept away in the crowd, gone perhaps for ever.

Lina showed me round the actual site, which is roped off, and introduced me to her colleagues, who looked at me with undisguised curiosity. Some friendly, some evidently wary. The site is apparently only just beginning to yield up its secrets, and will go on doing so yet for many years. Lina and I sat on a large stone in a neighbouring field of weeds and wild flowers, and I held her slender hand and thanked her for listening. She said she would like to talk again, and we shall, tonight, when we dine together once more.

30 August

We talked during dinner, how we talked. I did not know I had so much to say. That Lina is German seems to make it easier not harder. I asked her gently where her father and brother died and, as soon as the question was asked, my heart pounded for I suddenly realised what the answer might be. I prayed that we had not been in the same place at the same time, and that prayer was heard.

Both of them died at Passchendaele, in different regiments, on different days, a mile or so apart. And neither had known that the other was close by. War separates friends and families in many different ways. It took friends from me, close friends; deep friendships quickly made, and more quickly broken. I sometimes still feel it is worthless to begin a friendship, one might as well travel through time alone. For I learnt then that at least in that manner one avoids the pain of death, the hurt of loss.

I asked Lina hesitantly if she had heard of the Somme but, of course, she had. How could anyone alive today, English or German, not know that name? I told her I was there, one of the few fortunates who survived, but as I did not wish to talk at that time, we ate. We agreed I would tell her another time, so the evening should not be wholly sombre.

Nor was it, for we laughed a great deal as I recounted tales of my family, and of the rather stuffy life we lead in England. Lina agreed readily to help me in composing for my father a detailed letter about Epidavros, to confirm to him how my classical studies continue.

The meal ended with coffee and fruit, and after a liqueur at a bar down by the harbour, where with the lights of the night the black water rippled as if glow-worms swam bobbing beneath the surface, I walked with Lina back to her boarding house a few hundred yards from the café where we drank our liqueur. As we arrived at the unlit front door, holding hands, we said nothing. But Lina smiled as she opened the door and, keeping my hand in hers, led me through the entrance into the building's hallway. I closed the heavy door, which plunged us even farther into darkness and, in this Stygian gloom, I pulled Lina back to me and found her mouth and kissed her.

What a joy it was to feel a woman's lips on mine, to run the tip of my tongue over the soft inside of her own lips. I met the yielding resistance of her own tongue, a moist hot muscle pushing against me, then relaxing and allowing me in. I kissed every inch of her face, and she mine murmuring endearments the while, till she said softly 'Come,' and led me with whispered warnings up the creaky stairs and along a dark corridor to the secrecy of her own small room.

Lina told me to stay by the door as she moved in the darkness. Then I heard the rattle of matches, the scratching hiss of one being struck and the lamp was lit to bathe the tiny room in a warm glow. Not wishing to break the mood but knowing that practical matters had to be settled, I held her to me and told her that I was without protection; though I could return to my own room for a sheath if she wished. Lina said with an amused smile that it did not matter, she had brought some from Germany and would be glad not to take back the box unopened. Reaching into her bag beneath the bed, she placed her packet on a side table.

As we kissed again, I pressed my hardness urgently against the soft mound between her thighs and ran my fingers down her quivering back till they cupped her bottom and felt her contours through the dress. I kissed the nape of her neck, where wisps of blonde hair escaped from where the rest was pinned, and she forced her hand down between us to rub slowly against my hardness. Then she carefully undid the buttons of my trousers and sank to her knees before me, to take out my swollen shaft and place its head full into her mouth. The sensation was glorious.

Lina held my shaft with her two hands and slowly worked the head in and out of her mouth, licking it with her tongue. My legs truly felt weak as I lost myself in excitement of feeling and gripped the back of her head with my fingers. She stayed like this for some time, running her tongue round beneath my shaft, and caressing its sides till I felt it was about to come, when she once again took me deep into her mouth and sucked until the top almost burst with pleasure.

I made her stop, not wanting to climax so quickly. And she undressed me, removing my trousers and peeling back my shirt, while she still knelt before me, pausing only to run her tongue over the ridge of scar on my thigh. Then, when I was naked, she stood and I began to take off her clothing, ready to linger over each garment, revelling in every inch of the pale flesh to be revealed.

Unbuttoning the front of her thin blouse I saw a tight silken garment beneath which her generous breasts were visible, her nipples already erect. Any thoughts of lingering disappeared and I tugged impatiently at the straps, so that her rounded breasts shook gently as I pulled the under-garment from them and revealed Lina, naked to the waist, her soft skin fair and freckled.

Her breasts were indeed firm and full, and they moved with every motion she made. Lina raised her hands behind her head, which also tautened her breasts, so they appeared even higher and fuller, as she removed the pins from her hair and let it tumble to reach beyond the ends of her breasts so her nipples jutted through the long tresses of blonde hair.

I undid the remaining pearl buttons of her dress and slid the rest of her clothing to the floor, now kneeling before her as she had knelt before me. I pressed my face to the wisps of downy blonde hair that grew between her legs, and they felt soft as fern fronds against my face. I kissed her mound, inhaling the female scent, and I could see that already her moist lips were not fully hidden from view but had swollen and opened, like two curving ridges beneath her skin.

I fastened my lips hungrily on those ridges, and Lina sighed as I pushed my hot tongue along her furrow, and spread her legs wide so that I could reach the full length of her. Kneeling almost beneath her, I pushed up with my probing tongue, up and inside her. Then taking the lips of her quim between my lips, I sucked them into my mouth, which caused Lina to moan deeply and clasp her spread fingers against the side of my head, pulling me harder into her so that I could scarcely breathe.

My mouth was filled with her, the hair and the skin and the wet lips, and I rubbed my face against her quim, harder and harder, till I knew she was reaching her climax, then I quickened the licks and flicks of my twisting tongue till I felt her whole body tense to a long shudder and heard a moan that came from the depths of her pleasure. At that I stopped my movements, and pressed my head against her soft stomach in silence, feeling the tremors of joy rippling through her and slowly subsiding.

Lina fell back on her bed and told me happily in brief breathless words how good it had been. I lay down beside her and we curled up together, her back against me, her rounded buttocks pressed against my thighs. My half-erect penis snuggled into the warm crevice between her legs and grew hard again as I felt the hair and wet lips against it.

We lay like that for some time, till I began a gentle rocking which rubbed my shaft against the start of her lips and she responded.

I tried to insert myself into Lina without breaking my hold on her shoulders, forgetting precautions. But her entrance was too far forward and, instead, she turned round and reached for a sheath from the side-table. This she pressed over me, then sitting above me, straddled my shaft and held her heels with her hands, bent back so that my every movement pressed against the front of her quim. It heightened my pleasure to be able to see my member slide into her, to see her moist lips grip each side of me and feel her muscles reluctant to let me go.

I held her full hips tightly and moved her up and down over me, watching her taut breasts as they, too, moved to my rhythm, which grew faster and faster as I drew closer to my climax and, though I tried to slow so that Lina too would be ready, I failed and spurted deep inside her.

When I had finished, and knowing that Lina had not been satisfied, I asked her to lie on her back against me again, curled together, and this time I reached my hand around her waist and placed my fingers inside her, finding her moist pearl, which I touched and caressed until she reached her own climax, and grabbed my wrist to stop me fingering her at the same time as she yelled and bit into the pillow. . . .

So we stayed. And we were so close it was as if we slept each other's sleep.

At some time in the night I got up and turned off her lamp, but otherwise slept well, and woke in the morning to find Lina's sleeping head on my chest, an expression of angelic innocence on her face. Her eyes were tight closed, but her lips appeared to have a half-smile on them. Such vulnerability, to be asleep in the presence of another who is awake.

When Lina's sleep ended, she made no move other than to look up into my eyes and smile, and we dragged ourselves out of the night and into day by tender talk. In the light of dawn, as we lay naked and murmured to each other, I felt as if I was talking with thoughts, such was our intimacy.

Perhaps because of her own losses, I told Lina as I had told no-one before of that awful July morning when we prepared ourselves before stumbling up into the unknown, which turned out for most of us to be a hail of machine-gun bullets and shells.

I told Lina how James and I went out of that squalid trench together, ready to face anything; and how that hum of bullets which scythed down almost every man, virtually cut James in two, so that he was held together only by strands of torn flesh, and how he looked at me in shocked surprise as he fell, mouthing silences. And by the time he hit the ground I had already felt the burning within me, and wondered if the same were happening to me, and what it would feel like to die. But die I did not, though I felt the pain spread up into my gut as I lay there and watched James die, and saw that bewildered look still in his eyes as he stared at me, willing me to do something for him that I could not.

I could not move, nor look away either, but watched instead as his bent fingers twitched and clawed at the earth and blood flowed from what was left of his body, taking with it pieces of torn gut as he turned and the wounds opened even wider. His body disintegrated in front of me while his mind stayed alive and knew full well what was happening. I could not avoid his gaze, dare not look away and deny him one last brief contact: until eventually I realized the body was still, and the eyes would gaze in my direction forever.

I will not hide the fact that I cried as I described that moment, and Lina held me to her and I took comfort in the closeness of her body and in her warmth and kindness. Lina asked what had happened to me, so I told her that in time stretcher bearers had come and dragged me onto a stretcher, that I passed out for hours, then awoke as an old nurse wound a ragged bandage roughly around my thigh. She told me gently how lucky I was, that I had lost a great deal of blood, but that a bullet had passed clean through me, missing arteries and bones ... and missing my penis by a brief matter of inches.

I would rather have died that have that happen, as I had seen it happen before to others, who lived crippled like eunuchs and sentenced to a loveless life. Had I stumbled or come out of that trench in a different way, or simply hesitated and turned to look one way or another, then my fate could have been that of those other unfortunates, and I would never have known the pleasure of lying with a woman, the most joyous pleasure that I have known.

It is hard to know what to make of life. Chance decreed that James would die beside me, while I would survive comparatively unscathed. A few months' recuperation and I was back in action, living merely to survive each day.

In preaching against the war, I am not a coward. I have proved that when it comes to courage I am as brave as the next man – but the next man is dead, and that I will never forget. And I will take my pleasures innocently on every occasion, until I have had my fill ... and then I shall have more, so that my life overflows with them.

1 September

This morning, when we awoke, our legs were entangled so we made love lazily, and then dozed and let another day begin. Lina was to catch a later bus out to the site, as she had first to buy supplies – paper and such for the site records. While we waited for the shops to open we enjoyed a leisurely breakfast, waiting for our bread while the café owner sent his young boy running to the bakers to collect the day's batch; and when it came to the table it was deliciously warm, the pat of butter melting in its soft folds. With a cup of dark coffee and a tumbler of freshly-squeezed orange juice to complete our feast, and the sun just beginning to warm the day, I must have glowed with the pleasure I felt at being alive.